WITCH WAY TO GO

WITCH WAY TO GO

THE WITCH NEXT DOOR™ BOOK TWO

JUDITH BERENS

WITCH WAY TO GO TEAM

Thanks to the JIT Readers

Dave Hicks
Dorothy Lloyd
John Ashmore
Deb Mader
Jeff Eaton
Daniel Weigert
Peter Manis
Paul Westman

If we've missed anyone, please let us know!

Editor
SkyHunter Editing Team

From Martha

To everyone who still believes in magic
and all the possibilities that holds.
To all the readers who make this
entire ride so much fun.
And to my son, Louie and so many wonderful friends who
remind me all the time of what
really matters and how wonderful
life can be in any given moment.

From Michael

To Family, Friends and
Those Who Love
To Read.
May We All Enjoy Grace
To Live The Life We Are
Called.

ONE

"There's no way it's this easy." Lily's 2002 Winnebago Adventurer rolled slowly down Iliff Avenue in Lakewood, Colorado.

Beside her in the passenger seat, Romeo chuckled. "You know, it's totally okay to accept that something's going your way. If it's easy, let it be easy."

She kept her focus on the street numbers as they crawled past. They were so close. "Yeah, I've basically done that since my mom got her big break. I let so many things be easy. I don't think following her clues and running from the witches who don't want me to find them is supposed to be one of those things."

"I don't think there are any real rules in this scenario, Lil."

She licked her lips a little nervously. "Maybe not. The witch in the gray suit who tried to fry me extra-crispy said, 'We're cleaning up loose ends.' He wasn't alone. And I know what it feels like when something simply isn't right."

She glanced at the number 17284 on the mailbox as they passed it. She was looking for 17546.

"I assume that was part of your training too, huh?"

Lily turned quickly to meet his gaze, a little surprised by the question. "What? No. That's...that's only me. The other stuff, though—all the puzzles and coded messages. My mom's magic lessons turned into games. They definitely help."

"They got us into that speakeasy in Montreal, at the very least." Romeo wrinkled his nose and shook his head. "Part of me wonders what the heck they were doing in there with all those rooms. The other part of me..." He shrugged.

"Yeah, I'm not so sure I even want to know. Merely because an underground club has the Order of North's sigil on the front door doesn't mean it attracts the best of us. It's safe for all magicals but only recommended if you're a little crazy."

He snorted. "You saw that one witch with the ferret, right?"

"Yes. I saw the ferret and I'm sure it was staring at me." She shook the image out of her head and eased her foot on the gas barely enough to keep them moving forward. "Hey, what's that address on the corner?" She nodded toward the passenger window, and he leaned forward to squint at the house at the end of the street.

"17533."

"Okay. It should be up here on the left, then." They crossed Dover Court, and she slowed down more. "17542... 17544... What?" She pulled the Winnebago to the curb on the right side of the street and stared across Iliff at the house they'd been told to find.

Romeo took a deep breath through his nose and ran a hand through his dark curls. "Well, you were right about that."

"Yes, this is definitely not easy. Why would Bentley send us here?"

"I have absolutely no clue." His hands thumped onto the armrests. "Do you wanna go check it out?"

"Absolutely." Lily turned the engine off, stuck the keys in her purse, and opened the driver's door. Once she'd slid over the huge step onto the street, she turned to close the door behind her and stopped.

Her companion was already halfway through the process of half-jumping, half-sliding over the top of the incredibly wide center console between the front seats. He reached the driver's seat and scrambled out onto the asphalt. "You have no idea how badly I've wanted to do that." He grinned. "It's as awesome as I thought it would be."

Lily simply stared at him. "Okay, Hardcore Parkour. Now, it's outta your system, so we can put that behind us, right?"

"Oh, come on. You were sliding all over the new hard-wood with me."

She put a hand on her hip and tried hard not to laugh. "Last time I checked, those bamboo floors we put in are meant to be walked on. I've never seen a center console used as a jungle gym before."

He wiggled his eyebrows. "You have now."

"Romeo?"

"Yeah."

"Please don't make me put that awful carpet back in the Winnie."

His eyes widened over the ghost of a smile. "You wouldn't."

Lily raised an eyebrow in challenge, then turned and headed across the street. He jogged a little to catch up with her and they stepped up onto the sidewalk and stopped. A single-story home stood in front of them, built exactly like all the others in this neighborhood, or so they assumed. It was hard to be sure given the fact that it was black, charred, and almost burnt to the ground.

The first clues her mom had left her before she disappeared—and the rest of the world thought her dead—were a business card and a broken piece of metal Lily found in the single box of personal mementos she'd been allowed to keep. The bank had taken absolutely everything else, and even though she felt in her bones that Margaret Antony's will was a total fake, she no longer had the money to prove it.

The business card had led her and Romeo to *Le Chapeau Magique* in Montreal. They'd only been able to identify the broken metal after she reunited it with the other half in the club owner's office. She reached into her purse now and fingered the restored keyring charm in the shape of a maple leaf, which had once been attached to the club owner's keys that unlocked an invisible cabin on a lake in Canada's Mont Tremblant National Park. "Okay, the note I found in that trunk said to ask Bentley about four-fifty-two," she muttered. "And he gave us an address. I'm reasonably certain that address wasn't supposed to be destroyed in a fire."

"Do you think he knew about this when you called?" Romeo asked and squinted at the blackened husk in the half-acre lot.

She shook her head firmly. "No. I've known Bentley my whole life. He and my mom are still really close. He wouldn't have left something like this out if he knew—especially if whatever happened here keeps us from finding four-fifty-two."

"Whatever that is." He widened his stance and folded his arms. "He must have thought we'd arrive at this address and find a normal house in a normal neighborhood. That obviously didn't happen. There's no way anyone still lives here."

"Well, he didn't give me a name. Only the address. Maybe it's not about who lived here. Maybe it's what's inside the house that's important." She turned to look at him and raised her eyebrows. "What might still be there."

"It sounds like we need to—"

"Go in and look around? Definitely." Lily set off down the cement walkway that ran through the middle of the yard.

"Yep. Okay," he muttered behind her. "We're still on the same page."

The grass and a veritable forest of weeds almost covered the walkway completely. "The fire must've happened a while ago. I wonder why nobody came to clean the place up." The front door hung off its hinges, splintered and fragile-looking, but most of the house's support beams seemed fairly stable. Thankfully, the two steps onto the front porch were cement, and so was the porch. They wouldn't have to worry about falling through burnt and crumbling timber until they were inside.

"I bet I could simply take the whole door off," Romeo offered and studied the black rectangle of wood hanging sideways by one hinge.

"Yeah. Werewolf strength definitely comes in handy." She grinned at him. "Okay, before you unleash the beast, I need to do something first."

"Like what?"

Lily gestured toward the empty street and the neighborhood around them. "It's eleven in the morning on a Monday. If we're not careful, the whole neighborhood's gonna see you ripping doors off a burned house and both of us trespassing in broad daylight."

He tilted his head and studied her. "Wait. You're not talking about...time travel. Are you?"

A surprised giggle escaped her. "What?"

"You know. Speeding things up so we get to nighttime faster than everyone else. 'Cause if you can, my dad just lost a huge bet."

"Romeo." Grinning, she raised her eyebrows and waited for him to tell her he was joking. He didn't. "You and your dad made bets about me?"

"No, not you specifically. Merely witches in general. Julian Stephens doesn't believe in any kind of connection between magic and time travel."

She clapped her hands over her mouth to hold back a

shout. Her fingers raised long enough for her to whisper, "Time travel?" He shrugged. "I wouldn't settle your bet yet."

"But I'm right?"

Lily snorted and scrunched her eyes shut. Then, she gave his arm a reassuring rub. "Simply because I don't know anything about time travel doesn't mean it doesn't exist. But that's not remotely close to what I had in mind."

He looked genuinely disappointed. "Bummer."

"Sorry." She stared into his green eyes for a little longer before she patted his arm. "Stay here, okay? This won't take very long." She turned and walked a little closer to the sidewalk. With a deep breath, she closed her eyes and nodded. "Okay. Let's try this again. No black cloud this time, huh?"

She clapped her hands together, summoned the illusion, and drew her palms apart again in front of her chest. A thin, glistening purple film spread between them like she stretched a roll of violet tulle between her hands. When she'd spread her arms fully, the spell rose above her head and arced over her and the house. The shimmering purple veil fell all the way to the grass to encompass the entire property and formed a huge dome around it. The late-morning sun cast a light violet hue onto everything, but it wasn't much darker on the inside than on the outside.

Satisfied, she turned to face Romeo and dusted absolutely nothing off her hands as she returned to him and the cement porch. "That's what I meant to do in *Le Chapeau Magique.*"

"Instead of that giant black-cloud thing?" He stared at the purple dome with wide eyes.

"Yeah. I have no idea what that was. I'm good at illusion charms."

"I know."

"It's weird, though. I did everything exactly the same, and instead of an illusion, I unleashed this crazy...violent cloud of—"

"Lily?" She looked up at his gentle smile. "I know."

"Right. Sorry. But I really don't like having a spell backfire on me. That's only happened maybe two other times, but I realized what I'd done wrong the minute I cast them. That cloud, though—hmm?"

Romeo's hand now rested lightly on her lower back to get her attention, and he tilted his head toward her. "Can you guess what I'm about to say?"

She sighed and laughed at herself simultaneously. "You know." He nodded. "Okay. Point taken."

"Good. So, this spell of yours is gonna keep people out, right?"

"Only if they don't try to get in."

He bit his lip. "That doesn't really sound like keeping people out."

"Well, it's not. Technically. But what everybody out on the street sees right now—if they're even looking—is exactly what we saw when we pulled up. You can pull the doors off their hinges all day long and the nosey neighbors won't feel inclined to call the cops."

"Huh. That's actually good."

"Thank you." She gestured toward the lopsided front door. "Your turn."

With one more awed glance at the purple illusion, he scratched the back of his head and approached the doorway. Warped wood and rusty metal squealed for a few brief seconds, but the entire door detached in one pull. It also split in half down the middle and toppled out of his hands onto the cement porch in a spray of soot. With his arms still suspended in surprise, he glanced at her. "Okay, that was bound to happen anyway."

Lily stepped toward him, grabbed his forearm with both hands, and stood on her tiptoes to lean toward him. "Or maybe you're really strong." She left a quick peck on his cheek, dropped back onto her heels, and stepped through the doorway.

"I can't tell if you're joking or not."

She shrugged and fought back a laugh. "I think it's a little bit of both." Romeo snorted and followed her inside. They moved slowly, testing the charred floorboards beneath their weight.

"Hey, most houses in Colorado have basements, don't they?" he asked.

"I have no clue." The floor right beneath her next step looked like the timber had sunk a little under her slight weight, so she moved her foot to the right. It felt a lot sturdier there. "But it would make falling through the floor a much bigger problem."

"Yep." He moved through what had been the entry hall with her, his arms only half-raised as if he didn't want to look stupid holding his arms out for balance. "So don't fall through."

"Right back atcha." She looked at the burned ceiling. Most of the plaster had fallen away but some of it was still stained with uneven brown streaks that faded into black. The living room was surprisingly empty, probably because whatever furniture had filled it now existed as twisted heaps of ruin. They passed the kitchen, where both the blackened fridge and the soot-covered stove looked like they'd been smashed repeatedly with a sledgehammer. "Can a fire trash appliances?" she asked.

Romeo looked at her, and she gestured toward the kitchen. Squinting, he studied the damage. "Maybe if there was an explosion. Then again, I haven't really spent a lotta time in barbequed buildings."

"Right. You know, it looks like the fire could've been an accident. Except for the kitchen. Honestly, those dents in the fridge look more like they came from a giant fist."

"Well, we tabled time travel. But do giants exist?"

Lily shrugged. "They used to."

"Really?"

"Yeah. If there are any left, though, they're definitely not in the US."

"Huh." He took a deep breath and raised his eyebrows. "Hey, you know what the smell of charred house almost covers up?"

"Do you smell magic in here?"

"Yep." He sniffed again and nodded toward the small dining room on the other side of the kitchen. "That way."

"It's still so cool that you can do that. I have to use magic to find magic. All you have to do is be a werewolf."

He snorted. "Oh, yeah. That's all. It's super easy, by the way."

She stepped gingerly toward the dining room after him. "No, I didn't mean it as a bad thing. I watched you sliced with a nasty attack spell. Then you were shot—with a real bullet." She paused. "It was terrifying both times, but you simply popped right back up like nothing happened."

His eyes closed and he sent her a slow smile. "I wasn't trying to scare you."

"Oh, I know. I'm really glad werewolves have that fast-track to healing."

"You and me both, Lil." He winked and they moved on.

Two rectangular patches on the dining room's back wall were almost white against the peeling black of everything else. "It looks like someone took down a few pictures," Lily said.

"What?" He turned to see for himself. "Maybe we're not the first people to loot the place."

"We're not looting."

"Uh...we've stepped onto someone else's burned-down property without permission to look through the wreckage for a clue and maybe even more money your mom might have left here, which is totally still possible. And we found the place by reading a hidden message in a treasure chest at a lake. All we need now is a ship, and we're basically pirates."

Lily's mouth fell open. "Wow. That's a completely different take on things."

With his gaze fixed on the floor, Romeo skirted what had to have been the dining room table. "I think it's awesome."

She laughed. "I suppose Pirate Witch does have a certain ring to it."

"Yeah, you should get those boots that come all the way up to your—oh, hey. Look at that." He pointed briefly at the corner and she had to stand beside him in order to see it.

"So there is a basement after all."

"Yep. And it smells like the magic's coming from there."

"Then that's where we'll go. First, though, finish what you were saying about the boots."

Romeo looked a little awkward for a moment, then cleared his throat and grinned. "All the way up past your knees."

"Uh-huh."

"The Pirate Witch could totally pull it off."

"You know, it's an interesting thought. I'll keep it in mind." She stepped toward the open entrance to the staircase out of the dining room and looked into complete darkness. "Here's to hoping for no surprises."

TWO

"You know, I'm really glad fires don't generally burn downward." Lily moved slowly down the wooden stairs into the dark basement.

"Water does, though." Romeo's voice was flat and muted behind her.

"What do you mean?"

"Can't you smell that?"

"Nope."

He took another deep sniff. "Smoke and burnt wood upstairs. Mildew down here and magic everywhere."

Lily tilted her head in concentration and slid her foot slowly across what was now the cement basement floor to be sure she hadn't missed the last step. "Those could be song lyrics."

"Sure. If either of us were musically talented."

"Hey, I shake a mean maraca. Do you think there's a light switch down here?"

"I wouldn't even try." He sucked in a quick breath.

"House fires and electrical problems tend to show up together."

"Right." She raised her palm and summoned a yellow light orb, which she sent toward the ceiling of the basement until it lit the entire room. "Woah."

The unfinished basement was a wreck.

"That explains the mildew." Romeo's nostrils flared under the yellow glow of her spell.

Thick streams of water had dried on the stone foundation that ran halfway up the walls. The top half had been left open to expose the pink fluff of insulation that was now stained a sooty gray. Her spell light hovering below the ceiling illuminated the numerous water rings above them, and parts of the ceiling had buckled and warped beneath whatever water had collected there. Dry, caked marks of mud and soot smeared across the cement floors.

"A fire and a flood?"

He frowned as they made their way along opposite sides of the long basement that spanned the length of the house. "If the fire department was called, then yeah. They stopped the fire from spreading. I'm sure no one was too worried about flood damage at that point."

"But going through someone's stuff and tearing the place apart isn't in a firefighter's job description. So who did this?" Lily peered at a large metal filing cabinet that had toppled onto its side. The drawers were dented and halfway off their runners and the papers inside had been ruined by water and dried again in wrinkled shapes. A few loose scraps and folders lay scattered across the floor where they'd apparently been discarded. A broken lamp had obviously been thrown into the corner, thankfully unplugged.

Romeo walked through the upturned trunks, chests, and totes on his side of the long room. He leaned toward one filled with blankets, took a quick sniff, and jerked his head back and made a face. "Yeah, all this stuff is ruined. Whoever came through here was looking for something really specific."

"Let's hear your theory." She turned away from the filing cabinet and the fallen stool missing two of its four legs to face him as he lifted a tatty tarp. Under it, canned beans and tuna, bottled water, boxes of packaged crackers, and instant soup mix had been stacked.

"My guess is they weren't homeless. And they didn't need furniture." He nodded at the teak coffee table, stained with water rings and ash but otherwise in great condition. "I saw a box of jewelry on that bookshelf. It's still totally full."

"So whoever it was that came down here was looking for a different kind of valuable."

"Yeah. Like the magical kind." He flashed her a quick glance and shrugged. "Honestly, I can't tell where the magic is, Lil. This stuff's been down here for so long, it's all dust and mold and—" He uttered a disgusted grunt and stepped away from something at his feet.

"What is it?"

"A dead mouse."

"Gross."

"You're tellin' me. It looks like it's about to pop."

Lily stepped toward him for a better look, then shook

her head. "We need to get back to the source of whatever magic you said you smelled. It's still down here, right?" He nodded. "All right. I'll find it." She balled a fist against her chest and cast the exact opposite of her illusion spell outside around the deserted house. Another yellow light glowed in her palm, but this time, she concentrated it over the collection of random junk deemed too useless for anyone else to want to take. "There's gotta be something in here."

The trunk of mildewed blankets lit up under her glowing hands they moved across it like a flashlight beam. From there, she moved to the plastic tote of photo albums and a few framed pictures, followed by the boxes that had been stacked but were now shoved over onto the floor. Only two of them stood upright, but they all had water damage and one of them spilled an endless supply of hair-bows and ribbons across the stained cement. She even moved to the high metal shelf against the far wall and scanned the rows of power tools, cleaning supplies, and finally, the open box of jewelry.

"Okay..." She frowned at the scattered junk. "You smell magic, but there's not even a simple charm on any of this." She turned impatiently and studied the unfinished room under the glow of her magical lightbulb. "That filing cabinet looks about as damaged as the fridge."

"So they were both knocked around a little."

"I wonder if the person who started the fire is the same person who went through all this stuff."

"Maybe." Romeo raised his eyebrows and nodded in

understanding. "Okay, you think they came down here looking for something special—"

"Something magical is my bet."

"Right. And when they couldn't find it, they set the house on fire. That's a serious temper tantrum."

Lily met his gaze and smirked. "Or a warning. Think about it. None of the canned food was touched, and that's all stacked neatly. Wait." She passed her hand—still glowing with the revealing spell—over the packaged food and the tarp, then shook her head. "There's nothing there. But the owner looked like a fairly neat person and those boxes don't look very neat—like someone pushed them over. But the water got to all of them, so they were already on the floor by the time the fire was put out."

"Man." The surprise in his voice made her glance at him. "Did your mom train you to be a detective, too?"

She snorted. "That definitely wasn't her end goal. But I did learn that solving a puzzle is easier when you can see all the pieces in front of you. Or most of them, at least. Plus, I've read all the Sherlock Holmes stories at least half a dozen times."

He chuckled. "Bet no one ever thought those would apply to real life."

With a shrug, she stepped away from the piles of stored belongings and out into the uncluttered center area of the basement. "Well, they definitely put you in the mindset to pay attention to everything. Even if it doesn't seem important."

"So, witch detective..." He laughed at her jokingly irritated glance. "What else have you put together?"

"Well, let's say the arsonist came down here first and couldn't find what they were looking for. They trashed the basement, then went upstairs and were still pissed. It might explain why they trashed the fridge and the stove. Then, they decided they'd light the place up and maybe scare whoever lived here into handing over what they wanted. But then..." Lily stood in the middle of the room and cast the same revealing spell with her other hand, held both palms out, and turned in a slow, thorough circle.

"Is there a hole in your theory?" He stepped quickly over the dead mouse and headed toward her.

"Maybe not. Someone came back here to take the pictures off the wall after the fire. What if that person's the one who cast whatever spell I can't seem to find?" She continued her search and moved methodically over everything. "Because they wanted it to be hard to find so anyone who came back would have to work really hard for it. Looking through all the boxes and stuff down here is obvious. And the opposite of that would be—"

"Hidden in a wall that's literally falling apart?" Romeo asked.

Lily scrunched her face in consideration. "I'm thinking more like something written in the air."

"Um...it wasn't really a suggestion."

She turned toward him, both hands raised toward the ceiling. "Romeo, there are nicer ways to ask me to—"

"No, I mean—" He caught one of her wrists and aimed it at the basement wall opposite the stairs. "I mean it's in the wall."

When the glowing light of her palm struck a huge rip

in the plastic cover over the sagging insulation, Lily's mouth dropped. "Oh." A green light glowed from behind the rip in the uncovered wall. She moved her hand a few inches to the left, and the glow disappeared. "Oh. Good catch."

Romeo squeezed her shoulder. "I have no problem being the Watson to your Holmes."

"That's... Our thing is a little different than that, but I appreciate the effort." He merely grinned at her, and she nodded toward the wall. "So there's our magic, then." Once they reached the source of the green glow, it only appeared again once she raised her illuminated hand in front of it. "It's actually a really great hiding place. Look at this stuff. It's falling out all over the floor. There must have been a hell of a lotta water to gunk it all up like this." She stretched toward the torn hole in the plastic.

"Well, don't touch it."

"Why?"

He raised an eyebrow. "Fiberglass, Lily. It feels like picking a bouquet of poison ivy. Hold on." He turned and headed to the tools on the metal shelf.

"You haven't actually done that, have you?"

"No. But I did get fiberglass down my shirt working on a construction site a few months ago. I almost clawed my own skin off." He returned holding a pair of thick nylon gloves and offered them to her. "If you have to touch it, at least put these on."

"Thanks. I wouldn't have even thought of that."

Trying not to laugh, he nodded and took a deep breath. "Yeah. I know."

Lily pulled one of the gloves on, and the glowing light in her palm faded beneath it. She used the other hand to illuminate the green light inside the wall and shoved her gloved hand through the tear in the insulation's plastic covering. A puff of fiberglass and a rank cloud of mold wafted out and drifted down onto the concrete floor while she dug around inside the damp pink fluff. Finally, she removed her hand. "There's nothing in there."

"Well..." Romeo stepped back from the mess and she pulled the glove off inside out. "What about Open Sesame?"

She raised an eyebrow. "I've never seen that in any spell or ward or hidden message—hey."

"What? What'd I do?"

She pointed at him with a smug smile. "You helped me find the last puzzle piece. The revealing spell only showed us where the magic was coming from. Not what it's for." The glowing yellow light in her palms vanished, and she closed her eyes for a few seconds to think. "Okay. I guess this is my version of Open Sesame." With one finger, she drew a huge circle in the air where the green light had appeared and pressed her palm against the space between her and the insulation.

A blinding flash burst toward them and made her companion take a hasty step back. When the glare faded, it left a wavering green film in front of the plastic covering. It resembled green mist before it began to come together into dozens of different shapes. Only a few seconds later, the witch and the werewolf stared at a message that hovered directly in front of them.

"Puzzle solved." He pumped a fist, then stopped. "Or...almost."

"'For those looking to reclaim their secrets.'" Lily stared at the large, curling letters that pulsed in the air.

"Yeah, that's the part written in English. What language is the rest of it?"

"I don't think it's a language."

Romeo scratched his head, his expression one of confusion. "Okay. Maybe not a spoken language. But those symbols have to mean something."

"You're right, but I don't—oh, my God." She put both hands to her cheeks and held her breath as she scanned the twelve symbols beside the message they both understood. "No way."

"I'd love to share your obvious excitement, Lil."

She glanced at him quickly and his wide eyes reflected the glowing green of the message they'd uncovered. "Sorry. It's only... I can't believe these are here right now. It's been so long since I've seen them." She took a deep breath. "Romeo, I think she was here. Right here. She had to have been here. And that means we're still on the right track."

"Oh." His eyes lit up when she grinned at him. "Wait, why do you think she was here?"

"These are hers. The symbols. Okay, it's another one of my mom's games, right? She used to write me these coded messages on slips of paper and hide them all over the house. Most of the time, it was on my birthday. Like a scavenger hunt, except if I wanted to know where to look next, I had to decode it all first."

"Your mom made up her own language?"

Chuckling in disbelief, she focused on the symbols. "Yeah, a language she constantly reinvented. She'd changed three symbols every year, so I always had to pay attention. It really threw me off when she added one to replace T-H."

"Okay, so what does it say?"

"It doesn't say anything." She shook her head. "These are numbers."

"Like...numbers that mean something?"

"Hmm. Not yet." She gave her hands a little shake, licked the tip of her index finger, and began to trace the numbers she recognized in the air beside the green secret message.

Romeo snorted. "Are you writing in the air with magical spit?"

"What? Oh. No, it's merely a...thing my mom does." Smiling, she returned her attention to the symbols. "It helps me focus."

"I'm suddenly imagining your entire living room in your house when we were kids. All of it lit up in different colors while you and your mom wrote out magic lessons and codes and licked your fingers every couple of minutes."

"Actually, that's a fairly accurate description."

"Right. Who needs smartboards and iPads when you can draw on nothing?" He waved his hand in a wild gesture, aimed his finger at her, and pretended to poke her in the forehead.

"Hey, maybe I'll teach you how to do it one of these

days. That werewolf in Montreal found a way to perform magic. I bet it would work for you."

He dropped his hand and looked more than a little uncomfortable. "Yeah, that was still super-weird. I wouldn't be surprised if he made some kinda blood pact for that extra perk."

"Huh. Well, the offer stands if we ever learn how he did it. But I should probably focus on this first."

"Right. Right. Hey, would it still work if I licked your finger?"

"Stop it." Lily shook her head firmly, her eyes wide as she translated the number of each of the twelve symbols shimmering in the air. Her heart pounded with the realization that they were so close. They had to be.

THREE

Half an hour later, Lily puffed out a huge, frustrated sigh and lowered her hand. "None of this makes sense."

"Still?" Seated on the floor now with his arms wrapped around his knees pulled up toward his chest, Romeo raised his head. "How long is it supposed to take?"

"Not this long." She raised her hands to rearrange the shimmering pink numbers she'd drawn beside her mom's symbols. "I've run virtually every equation I can think of that worked with this code, turned the numbers into letters, placed them in every possible position. There's no pattern. They don't make any kind of shape. It's merely—" A jingling alarm made her jump and spin toward him. "You really need to change your ringtone."

"Yep. I know. Sorry." He leaned sideways to reach into his back pocket, then rolled his eyes and rejected the call. "It's like those prompts to be put on the Do Not Call list are backward. I've pressed star four different times from this number, and they're obviously still calling me."

She didn't have anything to say about that. All she wanted was to decipher what the numbers meant. "What am I missing?"

He hummed thoughtfully. "It could be a phone number."

"Yeah, but a phone number doesn't have twelve digits."

"It does if it's for another country. You know." He wiggled his cell phone at her. "The little 'plus one' at the beginning if you were calling the US from somewhere else?"

Lily frowned. "But the first numbers are...oh, my God. It's a five and a two. Do you know what country that would be for?"

When he shook his head and shrugged, she merely huffed with excitement, dug in her purse, and yanked her phone out. "There's only one way to find out. Maybe you should thank those telemarketers."

"Definitely not."

"They gave you the idea."

Romeo stood and shoved his phone into his back pocket again. "I'll consider it a debt paid for annoying the crap outta me. You could give me the credit for that idea."

She dialed the numbers in the order they appeared as green pulsing symbols and glanced up from the screen to give him a coy little smile. "Yes. Please take all the credit on that one. I shouldn't have overlooked the possibility that they were numbers." When the last digit was entered, she took a deep breath. "Wait. What if it's my mom?"

"That would be awesome." He turned his head to squint at her. "But you looked terrified."

"I might be." She swallowed and blinked fiercely a few times. Lowering her phone, she stepped away from the green message in the air and shook her head. "Or what if it's the people who have her? Think about it. If she's still alive, someone had to take her. This could be like a ransom note. Or a trap. What if—"

"Hey, okay. Take a breath, Lily." His hands were warm on her arms, but she suddenly felt quite cold.

"I just...I don't want to screw this up. I have to get it right. Getting it wrong is obviously dangerous for all of us at this point."

"Because you've been, what? Training your whole life to be as good at magic as you are? You're allowed to make mistakes, Lil."

Her lower lip trembled. "Not with this."

"Okay. Come here." He stepped even closer and wound his arms around her for a warm, solid hug. Her breath heaved out of her in one massive sigh again his chest, but she didn't cry. She couldn't. "Look, it's far more likely for your mom to answer that call than anyone who's trying to hurt her. Or you."

"I appreciate the optimism. But there's no way you can know that."

"Do you think your mom would've simply given away the secret-code language she created for you growing up? It doesn't make sense. Even if someone forced her to write this, she could've easily left you an entire note telling you exactly what happened and no one would know but you."

His voice was gentle enough, but it felt like a gong being struck inside her head.

She released a long, slow breath. "You're right." Pulling away from his chest, she craned her neck to look up at him. "So totally right. Thank you."

"That's why I'm here."

Lily giggled. "To be right?"

"To be on your side." With a finger pressed lightly under her chin, he tipped her head back a little more before he stooped to kiss her. It was short and sweet but he immediately looked confused. "I realize a moldy basement in a burned-down house isn't the most romantic place for anything."

She raised an eyebrow. "Romance, huh?" He laughed and glanced at her lips again. "We might have to table the romance for a while."

"Yeah. You have a phone call to make."

When he released her, she looked at her cell phone, checked the number once more against the floating green symbols, and pressed the call button and put it on speaker. The first two rings broke up on her end, which probably had to do with being in a basement. Despite that, she didn't want to leave until she knew whether or not this lead would take her anywhere.

The line rang a third time, then a fourth, and finally, whoever she'd called finally answered. They merely didn't say anything.

"Hello?" Lily asked and shared a wary glance with her companion.

"Who is this?" It was a woman's voice, low and confident with just a hint of concern.

"I found this number in a tracer message in the basement of 17546 West Iliff Avenue. For those looking to reclaim their secrets?"

"How did you get that address?"

When she looked at Romeo, he nodded with a shrug for her to go ahead. "Bentley McClure. I'm looking for four-fifty-two."

"Hmm." The woman cleared her throat, followed by a long pause. "Who else knows you're there right now?"

"Another friend. He came with me. Other than that, it's only the three of us."

"And you're sure no one followed you to the house?"

"I'm certain we covered our tracks." That was all she could say, and she wasn't about to spill the whole story to a stranger over the phone who was already skeptical. Still, she had no way to know if the witch in the gray suit or anyone who worked with him had followed her there. She wouldn't know until they tried to kill her again.

"All right." The woman sighed, and a loud rustle like wrapping paper came through the line. "I'll give you another address. Are you ready?"

Romeo retrieved his phone and nodded. "Yes," Lily said.

The woman gave them geographic coordinates instead. "Meet me there outside Camargo the day after tomorrow. Eight p.m. This isn't something we can reschedule, so if you can't make it by then, I can't help you."

"We'll make it."

"Don't be late."

It sounded like the woman was about to hang up, so Lily quickly added, "Wait. Can I have your name?"

The woman paused again. "I'll see you on Wednesday." Without even a moment's pause, she ended the call, and Lily held her breath as she stared at her phone's home screen.

"Okay..."

"It's a start, right?" Romeo leaned toward her to catch her attention.

She nodded and slid her phone back into her purse. "Have you ever heard of Camargo?"

"Nope. It sounds like somewhere in the southwest. Hold on." He punched the address into his phone and groaned. "Well, I got the south part right."

"Where is it?"

He pressed his lips together and looked wryly at her. "Mexico."

"Mexico. Okay. There's nothing at all shady about going to meet a woman I've never met at a random address in Mexico. All this, of course, based off a phone number I found using my mom's code which I found in the basement of a house that was broken into and almost burned to the ground." She took a deep breath. "Right."

"There are two ways to look at this." He pocketed his phone again. "We could go with the creepy as hell aspect, knowing everything I've heard about parts of Mexico not exactly being the safest. And that we'd have no idea who we'll meet or what they want." He shrugged. "Or we could go with the fact that that number was probably left here by your mom or someone who knows her really well."

"It's basically a giant neon arrow sign to finding her," she muttered, her gaze fixed vacantly on the floor.

"Yep. Is it dangerous? Yeah, that's highly likely. Do we know anything about it? No. Is it something we can't handle?"

She looked at him with wide eyes, and the slow smile spreading across her lips was reflected by his. "Was that a rhetorical question?"

"It doesn't have to be."

"Good. Let's go to Mexico."

FOUR

Thankfully, the rest of the house held up long enough for them to get out of that basement and walk back through the main floor toward the now yawning front entrance. "I guess we should hope no one looks too closely at this," Romeo said as he stepped over the charred front door onto the porch.

"Seeing as the place still hasn't been torn down or repaired, the lawn's overgrown, and the basement's moldy and harbors dead mice, I'd say that probably won't be an issue. At least until we're far enough away that it won't make a difference."

"In Mexico." He grinned. "I haven't been there since I was a kid."

"When did you go to Mexico?"

"Uh…with my mom, actually."

Lily turned to meet his gaze and raised her eyebrows. "Oh. So a really long time ago."

"Yeah, I'm almost sure that was our last family trip before she died." When she paused on the walkway in the yard in front of the purple dome of her illusion spell, he stopped beside her. "I honestly don't remember much. Only that we were all really happy." He shot her a lazy, nostalgic half-smile.

"Is that gonna be hard for you? Like, remembering your mom there?"

"Are you kidding? I get to go with you this time. I don't think it gets better than that."

She bit her lip before she smiled, took his hand, and laced their fingers together. "You took the words out of my mouth." With one more glance at the street to make sure there weren't any cars or people passing to see them appear out of seemingly thin air, she raised her hand and gestured at the purple dome of her spell. Then, she clenched her fist and yanked it to her side. The illusion vanished, and she dragged him onto the sidewalk with her. "And, just like that, we're two people taking a walk through the neighborhood."

"Eh, I kinda like it that we're not two ordinary people, though."

She squeezed his hand before she released it to locate her keys. "What other people don't know doesn't change who we are." He chuckled when she winked at him, he opened the Winnie's side door, and she walked around the front to climb into the driver's seat. The engine purred to life and she pulled slowly down Iliff to put distance between them and the house they technically had looted. *In a weird, magical message kinda way.*

"All right. I need my navigator again."

Romeo grinned. "On it." In under a minute, he'd mapped their entire route. "Hey, are you hungry?"

"Yeah. Lunch sounds good."

"You know, I wouldn't normally know where to start with restaurants, but I worked with someone for a while who came out here to visit...I dunno, a cousin or something, a couple of years ago. He talked often about any number of things in Colorado, actually."

"What, like good restaurants?" She chuckled. "That's what we're lookin' for right now."

"Yeah, a few restaurants. Honestly, I think he only came out here to buy weed. It was right after they legalized it."

"Huh. That doesn't need to be one of our stops, does it?"

"What? No...uh, unless you want to."

"I'm good."

He chuckled and tapped his phone. "Okay. I trust the dude's restaurant recommendations, though. There's a place, like, ten minutes away he said was good. It's on a golf course."

Lily frowned through the windshield and chanced a surprised glance away from the road. "A guy you used to work construction with came here to buy legal marijuana and go golfing?"

"Exactly."

Her mouth dropped open before she nodded. "Well, okay. So where are we heading?"

"It's called The Den. You gonna go all the way down to Kipling Street and head west."

"Wait, is that left or right?"

Romeo laughed and pointed to the right in front of them. "Do you see those?"

"The big mountains? Yeah."

"Okay, we're up against the foothills but those are the Rocky Mountains. They are west for virtually the entire state."

She leaned forward to look to their right and gaze at the small rise of foothills that gave way to shadowy, snow-capped peaks miles and miles away, some of them hidden behind the lowest layer of clouds. "Well, that makes things easy."

He snorted. "Yeah, we don't have any of those at home."

"Nope. There are no mountains in Charleston. Honestly, I've always simply oriented myself by 17 to Mount Pleasant and the Connector to JI." She shrugged. "This is, like...no one even has to think about directions here, huh?"

"Probably not. It makes it easier for all the people who come here from the South for legal weed." They burst out laughing, and she didn't have to ask again before she made the right turn off Kipling to head west.

THE DEN AT FOX HOLLOW—WHICH was the official

name of the restaurant on the golf course—was actually a pleasant place to stop for lunch before they continued their trip even farther south. They found a table outside on the patio with an incredible view of the Rockies right there in front of them and gave themselves an hour for chips and salsa, club sandwiches, and raspberry iced tea.

"Okay, this almost feels like a vacation." Lily wiped her mouth with a napkin and watched the golf carts driving down the sidewalk in front of the clubhouse. The wind rustled through the cottonwood trees lining a small creek beside them, and birds chirped. The click of golfers hitting ball after ball on the driving range across the parking lot punctuated the low chatter of other people who spent their Monday afternoon lounging outside over a good meal.

"Why not?" Romeo slurped the rest of his drink before the server returned to their table and asked if he wanted a refill. He answered with a nod and a grin.

"Why not?" She turned back to look at him, her expression serious. "Because it isn't a vacation. We're looking for my mom."

"No, I know." He narrowed his eyes and studied her for a minute. "And I'm not saying that doesn't matter. Because that's what we're doing. All I'm saying is—thank you." The waiter brought him a full glass of tea and left again quickly. "Lily, I'm only saying that it's okay to enjoy some parts of this, you know? You're allowed to have a good time."

"I know that." She nodded a little reluctantly and took another bite of her sandwich.

"And neither one of us is gonna be any good to your mom if we don't eat, sleep, or stretch our legs between one clue and the next, right? Please tell me you wouldn't still want to put in ten-hour driving days if this were an actual road trip for fun."

"I wouldn't." She wiped her mouth again, swallowed, and sighed. "I've spent basically all my time for two months in that RV. A road trip for fun would have to be mostly pulling over in cool places and getting out. And..." She smirked. "Letting ourselves get distracted."

"Oh, we can let ourselves get distracted whenever you want." He raised his eyebrows and jammed a few fries into his mouth. "But seriously. You know, out of all the things Julian Stephens taught me, it's that there's no point in doing anything important in life if you don't have fun sometimes."

"What?" She feigned surprise. "You mean your dad never drilled it into you that life is pain and no good deed goes unpunished, and success comes from hard work, dedication, and keeping your head down at all times?"

Romeo choked on his iced tea and struggled not to spray it across the table. "You—" He coughed. "You described my worst nightmare in clichés."

"Hey, maybe your worst nightmare is clichés."

"That's also possible."

Lily looked to watch a pair of mourning doves take flight from the trees beside the creek and flutter overhead toward the woods beside the driving range. "Well, at least they're not herons."

"What?"

"Oh." She pointed to the sky. "The birds. I know birds are everywhere and we can't really avoid 'em but I constantly think about the black heron and that shadow-bird...thing."

"The one that helped us cross the border into Canada with my magically faked passport?"

"Yeah. That one. I saw it first in the mirror the day we left, remember? Then over the lake when we stopped at that campground on the way. Mom taught me a long time ago that birds are some of the most symbolic creatures with a wider range of meaning than almost every other animal. So it's not really weird that they keep showing up. Only that I don't know what they mean."

He shrugged. "Maybe you're finding your spirit animal."

"Right. And we already know what yours is."

"Oh, ha, ha."

She grinned at him and bent her fingers into claws.

"Well, like you said. The birds here are definitely not herons."

Lily focused on a huge black crow that hopped onto the patio to peck at another patron's forgotten crumbs. Her eyes narrowed. "That definitely makes it much easier to believe no one's following us. Yet."

"Do you think they will?"

"Probably. That witch in Charleston wanted me dead. And we seriously pissed off the owner of *Le Chapeau Magique.* I can't pretend no one cares where we are or what we're doing."

"You don't have to." Romeo shook his head and leaned

back in the black-iron patio chair. "But that's exactly the kinda thing that makes it so important for us to let ourselves get distracted like you said." He eyed her sideways, the look suggestive. "Which is why I chose the coolest place for us to stop tonight."

"Oh, yeah?" Lily dipped a fry into honey mustard, popped it into her mouth, and pushed her plate away.

"Yeah. Santa Rosa, New Mexico."

This time, she was the one who almost choked. "How is that the coolest place?"

"Okay, fine. The coolest place that doesn't go that far out of our route."

"Which you totally already mapped out all the way to Camargo?"

"Exactly. And it's only six hours from here, so we can take our time. If we only have to meet mystery lady on Wednesday, we might as well do something fun." He pushed his chair back and stood. "I'm gonna go pay."

"Oh, here. At least take some—"

"Nope." He was already striding away toward the patio doors. "You covered virtually everything yesterday. It's my turn." He disappeared inside to head toward the bar.

She stared at the crow, which had now moved beneath the table beside hers to study a dropped blueberry warily. "Let myself relax a little?" she muttered. "I guess I can do that if it's my only option." The bird fluffed its wings and cocked its head. One black, glistening eye regarded her silently for a few seconds. "You don't seem to have a problem with that, do you?" Its head twitched again before it uttered a startling caw and burst into flight. She jumped in her chair and ducked beneath the glossy black wings.

"Birds—"

FIVE

The drive south through Castle Rock and Colorado Springs was gorgeous with the plains stretching endlessly on their left and the Rockies trailing beside them on the right. Romeo pulled up a folk band Lily had never heard of on his phone and played an album through the Winnie's speakers.

"I gotta say, I'm totally in love with having Bluetooth in this thing," he said and brandished his phone.

"I think having a new sound system in general wins first place on that one."

"It does sound amazing. You really weren't kidding about being able to find gold and diamond brokers almost anywhere."

"Yeah, I know." She glanced at him and made a face. "Didn't you believe me?"

"Well, I assumed you knew what you were talking about. The guy's eyes almost popped out of his head when you dumped those gold coins on his counter."

She shook her head but smiled at the memory. "It was definitely a good choice not to take the whole bag of them in there. And I like not really having a paper trail after Canada."

"There you go. There are so many pros to finding a bag of gold coins your mom left you in an old trunk and using it to fund our kind of secret...woman hunt?"

"That doesn't quite sound right."

"Okay, you're right. We'll figure it out eventually. Remember what I said about pirates?"

"Yeah, yeah. Hey, who is this?"

"The band? Elephant Revival. I thought I'd play some Colorado music. They're from here."

She nodded her head to the beat and what sounded like a fiddle above the guitars. "Is that a washboard?"

"Oh, yeah. She rocks the washboard—wears it on her chest and everything."

"Well, you can play them as long as you want to."

Romeo stared at her for a moment before he leaned back in his seat. "Are we getting closer to finding that theme song?"

"What?" Lily laughed. "I thought I'd already found it. Remember?"

"Oh, no. 'Back in the Saddle Again' isn't our theme song. And I'm sure you used Aerosmith as a wingman that night. I'm still weighing the pros and cons of that one."

"There were only pros." she winked at him. "And if you manage to play some song in a perfect moment like that for getting frisky in an RV... Well, I won't stop you."

He chuckled. "That's good to know." He placed his phone in the center console's cupholder, rolled down the automatic window, and raised his face to the dry, warm Colorado air that ruffled through his dark curls.

THE GREAT VIEW lasted only as far as Pueblo, where the Rockies diminished into comparatively smaller hills to the west. The east and south stretched out before them on I-25 as one flat, brown, dusty expanse of practically nothing at all. Lily frowned. "That was fast."

"What?"

"Beautiful drive turned badlands."

"Well, south for us is the ocean and beaches and marsh." Romeo swept his gaze across the nothingness. "On this side of the country, south is...desert wasteland."

"It has to get better, though, right? My mom had a few acquaintances, I recall, who constantly talked about how beautiful New Mexico was. And Arizona. There's no way they could have meant this."

"Probably not. We'll hafta get there and find out, huh?"

"I really hope this isn't the rest of the drive from here to Camargo. If I was religious at all, I'd probably say this was Purgatory."

He chuckled. "Well, if it is, at least you have me with you."

She stared at him with wide eyes until he laughed. Then, she returned her attention to the road and pressed on the gas a little, loving the fact that Colorado had high-ways with an eighty-mile-per-hour speed limit.

The desert began to change slightly once they reached Las Vegas, which they went through to get off on US-84. "Okay, I know this is Las Vegas, New Mexico, and not as big as the one in Nevada, but I'm sure it has its own version of hidden clubs for magicals," Lily said. "But I don't think I could handle any of that right now."

"I don't think I could handle it ever. Too many people. Too much...Vegas."

A little before 6:30 that evening, they pulled off I-40 into Santa Rosa Lake State Park. "Where's the lake?" she asked.

"It's...uh, a little north of the campsite." He scrolled through his phone.

"Where are the plants? We seemed to be heading toward mountains again. And, like...trees."

He snorted. "Okay, I expected more than this too. But hey, it's not desert and nothingness anymore. At least there's that."

With a laugh of disbelief, she shook her head and studied the stretch of road they still had to drive. "You're right. It's all rocks."

"I promise there's a lake."

"Okay..."

They did finally drive through a few coarse, dry-looking trees, shrubby and stunted and surrounded by prickly bushes everywhere. They might've been slightly green in color, but they merely looked like dots of black against the golden sand, rock, and parched earth. The RV campsite wasn't much better, either.

"To give you fair warning ahead of time, I won't turn the AC off for the night. I don't care if there aren't electrical hookups. We'll use the generators."

"Yeah, that's probably a good idea. I don't think it gets under seventy-five here. Ever. Including at night."

"With no humidity. It sounds like torture."

Romeo laughed. "How about it sounds like practice? By the time we get to Camargo, we'll have had two days of desert-like existence."

"Two?"

"Yeah, I thought we'd take our time tomorrow, drive to the border, and stop around El Paso. That'll break it into five-hour stretches. Unless you wanna drive for ten hours all day tomorrow and hang around in a town in Mexico while we wait for that meeting."

"No, that sounds like way less fun."

"Okay." He directed her to their assigned RV site, which did actually have hookups. They both got out to take care of that first before exploring their surroundings.

"I think you totally mastered the hookup, Romeo."

He plugged the final cord in, straightened from the electrical box, and turned to face her with a wink. "I seem to recall that happened a few nights ago."

"What? No, I was talking about literal RV hookups."

"Uh-huh." Grinning, he stepped toward her.

"I'm serious." Lily's mouth fell open in silent laughter.

"So you wouldn't say I've mastered both of them,

then?" He stopped so close in front of her, she had to tilt her head almost all the way back to look at him.

"Mastered... Well, first of all, I'm not a hookup."

"Very, very true." He slid his arms around her, pulled her completely against his chest, and kissed her so forcefully, it would have knocked her off her feet if he wasn't already holding her. When he finally pulled away, she took a sharp breath and bit her lip. "Any mastery at all, though? Even if we're not calling it a hookup?"

Laughing, she shook her head. "I choose not to answer that right now."

Romeo's green eyes glowed in the light that wasn't even close to sunset this far south. "Too soon?"

If she didn't know he was a werewolf, she would have called that grin of his startlingly feral. "No. But I'm really hot and sweaty and—"

"You're welcome."

She raised her eyebrows. "From the heat."

A deep, quiet laugh escaped him. "Uh-huh."

"You're really gonna keep pushing this, aren't you?"

"You haven't stopped me yet." He turned with her in his arms and headed toward the RV, forcing her to walk backward to stay on her feet. Her arms wound around his waist tightly.

"I'm sorry. Excuse me."

They released each other enough to turn halfway toward the woman who'd snuck up on them. "Hi," Lily said, her cheeks flushed from any combination of heat, excitement, and a little embarrassment.

The interloper grinned at them, her long gray hair

piled into a bun on the top of her head and bound in a bright yellow scarf. "I couldn't help myself." Her hands moved in huge circles as she spoke and the loose, flowing sleeves of her boldly colored paisley tunic fluttered around her arms. "I saw you two from our site, and I had to come over here and say you are both so beautiful. Truly. It is such a joy to see young couples out here, enjoying each other outside without constantly being plugged into technology. And you're on a road trip together. It's absolutely... it's perfect."

Lily pressed her lips together and glanced at Romeo, who looked like he was about to explode with laughter if she didn't say something. "Um...thank you."

"Oh, don't thank me. You just thank each other." The woman's hands fluttered toward them as if she were shooing them away after her odd interruption. "Listen, my name's Suzanne. My partner and I came out here with friends of ours for the week, and we're having a little gathering tonight at the lake." She turned a little to jerk her finger toward the only body of water around for miles. "We would love to have you join us. Have you been to New Mexico before?" The dozens of silver bangles on her wrists jangled when she clapped her hands and glanced quickly from Romeo to Lily.

"This is our first time," he replied, apparently in control of himself again. Lily merely nodded.

"Oh, that's so much fun. There are so many fantastic things about this place. It's truly magical."

"Really?" His eyes widened. While he'd probably masked his sarcasm fairly well from this Suzanne woman, his friend pinched the skin below his ribs and fought back a smile when he twitched against her.

"You have no idea. Now, I realize you just got here. You need time to settle in. Don't feel like I'm rushing you. But please, when you're ready, do come and join us. Have a few drinks, listen to some stories, and participate in anything that looks like fun. You'll have the best time, and I can tell simply by looking at you two that you will find exactly what you're looking for. I promise you won't be disappointed. Just...stop by." The woman practically leapt toward them and extended her hand for the other half of their introductions.

"Oh. I'm Romeo." He shook her hand to the repeated clink of so many bangles again.

"Lily."

Suzanne's eyes widened above a grin when she shook her hand next. "I'm simply... I'm delighted. So nice to meet you. Hopefully, I'll see you both in a little while."

"Sure." Lily smiled sweetly and nodded. Romeo wiggled his fingers in a hesitant wave, and the woman turned twice to grin at them while she hurried off, her hands clasped together against her chest. They watched as she caught up to an older man in shorts and hiking sandals, who'd waited for Suzanne much farther down the path toward the lake. He raised an arm in greeting, which they returned. They couldn't hear what she said, but Suzanne's voice rose excitedly as she flapped her hands and headed toward the lake. The man shoved both hands in his pockets and didn't seem to manage a word in edgewise.

"Wow." Lily couldn't seem to tear her gaze away. "That was…"

"Apparently, we're a beautiful young couple."

She smacked his chest. "Because a crazy old lady said it?" He simply shrugged. "That was one of the weirdest interactions I've ever had. What do you think that gathering is?"

He smirked cheekily. "Honestly, the first thing that went through my mind was swingers."

"What?" Lily barked out a laugh and covered her mouth hastily with her hand.

"We're having a gathering." He gestured with one hand and nodded his head. "Have a few drinks and participate in anything that looks like fun." He snorted. "That doesn't sound like a possible swinger party to you?"

"And what exactly do you know about those?"

His shoulders hunched in laughter. "Nothing, actually."

Lily returned her attention to the lake, where two more people had joined Suzanne with a huge plastic cooler carried between them. "What if they're all, like…her age?"

"It probably won't be a very late night, then."

She scrunched her face. "I don't know if that's hilarious or disturbing."

Laughing, he pulled her toward him again and leaned back against the Winnebago. "How about we eat first? Then we can decide whether or not to accept the invitation."

"Oh, jeez. You know, I'm actually kinda intrigued." She smiled playfully but it settled into an uncertain grimace. "For curiosity's sake, we should go. I really wanna know what the heck that woman was talking about."

"Okay." He chuckled. "And if any old dudes start hitting on you?"

"Please." He didn't stop her when she pushed herself out of his arms and stretched past him to open the Winnie's side door. "You have nothing to worry about. Trust me."

SIX

They made a simple dinner in the Winnie's small but completely functional kitchen using the few staples they'd bought at the grocery store before they reached Colorado—spinach salad with cherry tomatoes and cucumbers, which she'd made only for herself because Romeo refused to eat rabbit food and a frozen pasta dinner for two that they heated on the stove.

"I think I saw a few picnic tables outside," he said as he picked their plates up off the counter.

"First, it's way too hot out there to eat anything. Second, I have a feeling that eating outside would merely be another open invitation for Suzanne and her friends to barge in on our dinner." He snorted. "Hey, don't get me wrong. I like friendly people but not when I'm trying to eat."

"Fair enough." He set the plates on the small table beside the couch and slid into the booth. "Ow. Hey, can we put more legroom on the list of RV updates?"

She raised an eyebrow, sat across from him, and handed him a fork. "I didn't know we were making a list."

"Come on, there's always room for improvement."

"But not for your legs."

"Very funny, Lily."

Grinning, she dug into her salad while he failed at making an angry face.

***

When they stepped out of the Winnebago, it was almost 8:oo p.m. with considerable light left in the sky. "Okay, this is acceptable dry heat." Lily stared out across the open expanse of sand, rock, and shrubs while she waited for him to close the door behind him.

"Yeah, it'll probably cool off a little once the sun goes down. I think it gets up into the hundreds here. Like frequently, too."

"Mexico has more trees and shade, right?"

Chuckling, he stopped beside her. "You've never been there?"

She shrugged. "Only to Cancun and Puerto Vallarta. You know, five-star resorts on the water. That's not what Camargo is, though, is it?"

"Nope. It's totally landlocked and still hot. But it does have at least one lake and a few rivers. And it's right next to the mountains so I'd say it's a little better than this."

"Did you look all that up while I was driving?"

"Yeah."

"You know, I couldn't have found a better navigator, researcher, and trip-planner all combined into one."

Romeo smirked. "Please don't ask me to guide a tour."

She laughed. "Well not here, at least. I can see literally everything there is to see by standing in one spot." She glanced down briefly when he slid his hand into hers.

"Not Suzanne's gathering, though. That's still a surprise."

"Do you still wanna check it out?"

"The anticipation's killing me." Giving her hand a little squeeze, he pulled her gently with him away from the RV sites and toward the path to the lake. "She did say we'd find what we were looking for there."

"What, like my mom?" Lily couldn't hold a straight face for longer than two seconds. "I have absolutely no idea what she thinks we're looking for."

"Hey, if it's not there, we'll simply come back and have our own gathering. And we don't have to invite anybody to that."

"I wouldn't have it any other way."

The path rounded a bend obscured by the scrubby bushes that grew denser closer they got to the lake. The murmur of voices and a few ringing laughs rose toward them with a muted echo. A few steps later, the ground dipped a little toward the rocky beach and the gathering came fully into view.

"Wow. That's more people than I expected." Lily hesitated and stared, her expression wary.

Romeo raised an eyebrow and scanned the beach

where small groups were huddled in conversation. "How are they not louder?"

"Yeah, that's a little odd." They continued along the path until it petered out at the shore. A sharp tingle washed over her entire body and the full sound of this fairly large throng struck them full-force. "Oh." She chuckled. "This is also a magical gathering. They put up dampening wards."

He grimaced and shook his head. "I'm getting that *now*."

"Is the smell gonna bother you?" She looked at him with a sympathetic smile.

"It's not anything like that bar in Montreal, at least. Plus, there's fresh air here. I'll be fine."

"Okay. Well, let me know. Or you can always simply breathe through your mouth like last time."

"Yeah, that's a great way to make new friends."

Laughing, she gave his hand a few reassuring squeezes and they wandered toward the group of at least thirty people who had chosen Santa Rosa Lake for their little get-together. "It's funny how this is the second campsite we've pulled up to for the night that also just so happened to have a group of magicals there to party. If it happens again, I'd say there was a weird pattern developing."

"Well, witches like to enjoy their summers too, don't they?" Romeo winked at her.

"I don't need a witch party to enjoy my summer." She laughed anyway, then leaned against him and grasped his arm above their clasped hands. Suzanne had seen them and the woman now scampered over the pebbled beach, waving her arms, bangles and all.

"Oh, I am so glad you decided to join us! This is incredibly informal, as I'm sure you can tell. Nothing fancy at all. But the lake is gorgeous, and sunset makes it even that much more of a treat. Oh, and then—Fred. Fred! Come here." She gestured frantically.

The man they'd seen join her on the path now headed toward them, his eyes narrowed above the barest hint of a smile. "I see she roped you in. Fred Moesler." He thrust his hand out toward Romeo first, then Lily. After the introductions, his hands returned the pockets of his shorts again. "So, which one of you is...you know. Not human?"

"Um..." Lily glanced at Romeo. "Both of us."

The older woman clapped her hands together in delight. "Oh, you're both witches. That's so wonderful!"

She choked back a laugh. "Well, we're not—"

"Only Lily." He leaned toward Suzanne and lowered his voice. "I'm a werewolf." To make his point, he let that side of him out barely enough to make his eyes flash blazing silver.

"Oh!" Her eyelashes fluttered, her mouth dropped open, and she looked quickly from Fred to Romeo. "Oh, that's... I simply..." A cackle of glee burst from her mouth. "You're my first, then. I'm thrilled!"

Fred pressed his lips together and gave the younger man a single nod of solidarity. Beyond that, he looked entirely unaffected by anything else happening around them.

"I can't wait to tell the others we have a werewolf here

with us tonight." Suzanne's bright blue eyes sparkled in the fading sunlight.

Romeo tilted his head. "That...might not be—"

"No, no. It's absolutely fine." The woman's hands whipped wildly in the air. "These witches have had all types of magicals in their midst. Now, I'm well aware of the tendency of some witches to...well, discriminate, I suppose you'd say. But none of those are here with us tonight."

"Including yourself?" he asked. Lily looked at him and caught the tension in his jaw, although he looked relaxed enough.

"Oh, me?" Suzanne put a hand to her chest, then glanced at Fred. The man merely raised one shoulder in a half-hearted shrug. "Oh, no. No, Fred and I aren't witches. We're not magicals of any kind, I'm afraid."

"Really?" Lily tried really hard not to look as confused as she felt. "So how did you—"

"Become a part of all this?" The bangles jingled enthusiastically, and she tossed her head. "My parents were witches, actually. Everyone thought I would be too, but the magic skipped me altogether. I'm the first in at least eight generations not to have received even a trace of it."

"Oh." *What else am I supposed to say to that?*

The woman who wasn't a witch laughed. "Don't be sorry for me, Lily. Really. I can see a magical from a mile away. And I know my family's entire spellbook by heart. I merely can't perform any of them. But I've found there is a terrible lack of intermediaries between magicals and non-magicals. Not that the time for mingling the two is anywhere close to the present." She turned to look at her companion, then placed a hand on his chest for a half-hug. "My husband is my inspiration for even dreaming that it could be possible one day."

Fred turned to give his wife a quick kiss and tipped his head toward Romeo and Lily. "Simply another thing in this crazy world to get used to," he said. "If you're willing to be open to it. Honestly, I'd take magic and witches and the whole shebang over...well, hell, any number of things." Nodding, he looked at the few dozen gathered witches around them. "We have a good group of people here tonight. I'm glad you two could join us."

"Thanks," Lily said.

"So. Drinks are over there in those two coolers. We have a few party platters to munch on if you're feeling peckish. Enjoy yourselves and mingle for now. There's a drum circle later and a few other ceremonies I never tire of seeing. And if you have any questions or need anything, come find me." With a wiggle of her fingers, Suzanne linked her arm through her husband's and they wandered away to apparently make their rounds to the other smaller groups of people who could perform magic.

"I didn't know magic could skip a generation," Romeo said.

"Me neither. And I've never seen a human exposed to magic who didn't have their memory wiped with a charm afterward."

"I guess Fred's the man."

Lily laughed. "Yeah, he doesn't seem to think any of

this is as big a deal as his wife makes it out to be. I feel a little better about joining the party now."

"So they're definitely not swingers."

She rolled her eyes at him and walked purposely to the drink coolers. After rummaging through for a minute, she lifted two options. "It looks like spiked seltzer or...Yuengling."

"Beer."

Lily selected a pomegranate-flavored alcoholic seltzer for herself and together, they moved among the witches gathered in front of a lake in the middle of nowhere, New Mexico. Occasionally, they caught the gazes of a few witches who'd quite clearly heard from Suzanne that Romeo was a special guest tonight. After the first two or three curious glances, he began to lift his beer in a salute to anyone who paid him any attention at all.

"You're really enjoying this, aren't you?" She hid her smirk behind a long sip of her spiked seltzer.

"I'll take what I can get." He nodded at two men who held their drinks out toward him in passing. "I might actually be the only werewolf in the history of magicals who gets to be a celebrity at a desert witch party. I definitely do not expect this to happen again."

"Yeah, it probably won't." She smiled and nodded graciously when Suzanne turned from yet another group to point directly at them. "It's kinda fun, though."

"Oh, you're enjoying it, huh?"

"It's merely pleasant not to be in the spotlight for a change. After all the functions I went to with my mom... They made me uncomfortable, actually, as I got way too much attention simply because I was Greta Antony's daughter. That only changed once everyone thought she was dead."

"Hey, give yourself more credit." He slid his arm around her shoulders and pulled her closer. "You're a big deal even without being the famous professor's daughter."

"Well, right now, I'm gonna go ahead and let you take all the credit." She lifted her can and he clinked his against it.

"Aw. Aren't you sweet?" He kissed her temple and they both sipped in silence for a while.

Closer to the water, two witches stood facing each other, drawing symbols in the air to create a joint-effort pattern above the sand between them. Laughing, a younger woman in her mid- to late-thirties cast an animation spell that formed a dragon out of the dry, sunbaked sand. It uttered a tiny roar and strutted along the shoreline. Sand and pebbles scattered in its wake.

Lily raised an eyebrow at Romeo and repeated her own version of the spell. Her creation erupted from the sand as a giant crab that scuttled after the dragon and snapped at its dusty heels with massive claws. The witch who'd made the dragon looked up in surprise, then caught sight of Lily.

A grin spread over the woman's face and she spread her arms. "I guess we'll have to let them work it out, huh?"

Lily raised her drink, and the other witch laughed before she drained the rest of her clear plastic wineglass.

"This kind of entertainment definitely beats whatever they were doing in Canada," Romeo said.

"Oh, yeah. These people are actually having a good

time." She frowned. "The magicals in Montreal were simply..." She trailed off, unable to find quite the right word.

"Desperate?"

She chuckled wryly. "That's one way of putting it. Hey." She stopped abruptly, turned toward him, and caught his arm. "You were totally right about needing a little fun. To relax, right? And this actually feels... normal."

"Now you're getting it."

The high trill of a flute caught their attention. A man held a wooden flute to his lips, but he only played a few stanzas of the melody before he lowered the instrument again with a grin. The music, though, continued to play without him.

As the sun sank toward the western horizon and the mountains that looked so much smaller all the way out there, the desert around them took on a golden glow. The sky filled with purple, orange, and red, reflected intensely by the lake without anything to block the light. A man in a huge sun hat and hunched over his cane as it cracked across the pebbly beach with every step, made his rounds through the lakeside party. He waved his hand at everyone he passed.

Lily couldn't tell what he was doing until two small white votive candles appeared in front of her and her companion. Romeo almost choked on his beer when he flinched away from the item that had appeared without warning. "You okay, there?"

Laughing at himself, he nodded and pointed first at her, then the candle. "I can only assume those are for us?"

"I guess so." All the other witches around them took their candles from the air as each appeared and lit them with their own spells. She winked at him. "I got you." With a flick of her fingers, she lit both at once. "That was the first spell I ever learned, actually. It's one of the easiest."

He laughed. "Well, I wouldn't know what to do with it anyway."

"It looks literally like a kind of decorating, maybe." She gestured at the other witches around them, who'd more or less formed a loose circle. Some of them sent their flickering, floating candles to settle on the surrounding rocks or along the beach. Others merely lifted theirs high above the gathering.

"I feel like we're in a cave, now," he muttered.

She snorted and elbowed him lightly in the ribs.

The conversations continued around them, although the other witches' voices had slowly begun to die out. "Something's about to happen." She watched the others in search of the next big thing.

A huge explosion sounded beside the path from the campsite to the lake. She jumped and raised her hand, ready to throw a defensive spell as they both whirled toward the sound.

SEVEN

The witches erupted into boisterous shouts all around them. "What's that—" Lily's heart pounded in her chest. A second later, all her instincts settled into place once more and she threw her head back in laughter.

Romeo expelled a huge sigh and tipped his beer back. He swallowed, shook his head, and muttered, "They sure do know how to make an entrance."

"Well, Suzanne did mention a drum circle, didn't she?"

The cries rising from the gathered witches weren't in fear or surprise. They were, in fact, cheering.

Three men and two women formed a loose procession across the beach and moved toward the scattered circle of magicals. They didn't wear any type of uniform, costume, or identifying badges to mark them as belonging to any particular Order or other magical organization. But they were all relatively young—at least younger than the majority of the witches there—and all five of them had long, straight, bone-white hair. The explosion sounded again, now easily identifiable as coming from their drums.

Each carried large ceremonial drums of cowhide under one arm and pounded out the deep, echoing rhythms with their free hands. At the end of this line walked a woman almost as bent and crooked as the male witch who'd distributed the candles, although she didn't use a cane. Her hair was white as well, although it still had a blondish sheen to it. The huge presence she commanded sent a shivering trail of excitement down Lily's spine.

"This is incredible," she whispered.

"They can definitely keep an exciting beat." He shrugged and took another gulp of beer.

She looked at him. "That's true, but it's not what I'm talking about." He raised an eyebrow and sent her a small, curious smile. She took a deep breath and glanced at the drummers who now made their way into the large circle. "When I was a kid, my mom made a big deal out of telling stories, right? She'd build a fire outside and make up these random tales. Sometimes, she even conjured images to go with it. I thought they were simply a fun thing she liked to do, but when I got older, she said that magic and stories have always been intertwined. That there was a group of magicals out there whose job it was to keep magic alive by telling stories and vice versa."

"Like another Order?" Romeo had lowered his beer now to pay a little more attention to the drummers.

"Not exactly." Lily smiled to see him suddenly more focused. "More like a tribe. They're all over the world—in every continent and every country."

"That's a big family."

She giggled softly and tried to keep it low. "They're not related by blood. Only by story. They're born as story-tellers of magic, but it doesn't matter where they come from or who their families are."

"Hmm. How does that work?"

"Probably the same way not all witches or werewolves are related to each other."

He snorted and nodded after a moment. "Okay. I'm allowed at least one stupid question."

"It wasn't stupid. Honestly, it took me a while to wrap my head around it too. Whatever they're planning right now, I think it's about to start. You're gonna love this."

"I am ready to be amazed."

The drummers filed into the circle of witches, and the steadily quickening rhythm of their beat grew so loud, it would've been hard to continue any kind of conversation there. Two of the men closed their eyes as their hands flew over the stretched hide under their arms. The third man and one of the women stared intently at each other, clearly feeding off each other's energy to play off each drummer's slightly different rhythm—simply one part of the whole. The second woman had her head thrown back to the sky where the flickering light from all the candles that drifted above them cast dancing shadows over her face as she stamped her bare feet on the pebbled beach.

The old, hunched woman continued on her path behind the drummers and moved with the slowness of age but the confidence of youth. Her head nodded to the drumbeat, and as she passed the two young people, she raised her bowed head to look right at them. Milky white eyes stared into Lily's blue ones. Then, the old woman's blank gaze shifted to settle on Romeo's face. A second later, her mouth opened into a wide grin of pink gums and no teeth at all. A squeaking giggle escaped her, mostly drowned out by the drums, before she continued toward the center of the circle.

Romeo bent to whisper in Lily's ear. "Is she blind?" She shrugged, unable to take her eyes off the scene that unfolded slowly before them.

The old woman somehow made her way into the very center of the five drummers—a challenge as they stood close together and it seemed impossible that anyone could slip between them. They pounded louder and louder on their instruments and increased to an almost over-whelming speed. With a final, enormous burst even louder than the first beat marking their presence, the drummers fell silent and slid back across the beach, widening their tight circle as the old woman straightened abruptly from her crouch and threw her arms up toward the sky. Each of the musicians was now on their knees, their heads bowed and their drums tucked under their arms while their free hands rested on the small of their backs.

"That looked like a kung-fu movie," Romeo whispered in her ear again.

"Shh." Lily turned her head toward him but couldn't look away from the woman. His head jerked up at the sound of the ancient storyteller's voice.

"My kindred souls! Heirs of the Mother Moon and the Father Sun. Brethren of blood and magic and the breath of existence! Listen to my words." The drummers pounded another cracking, deafening boom from their drums.

Lily blinked and glanced past the old woman to the other side of the circle to meet Suzanne's gaze. The woman stood with her hands clasped at her heart and Fred's arm draped casually around her shoulders, raised her eyebrows at the younger woman, and grinned as she nodded toward the storyteller.

"We gather tonight in love and respect," the old woman continued, her arms still uplifted with surprising strength. "Toward ourselves and each other. Toward the world into which each of us has been called. Toward all those who have not stepped across its borders. And it is each of our responsibility to use what magic has given us to lift all of it into balance." Finally, she lowered her arms slowly to her sides again, and the drummers struck another slightly softer beat.

"We have received our gifts. Light." She jerked a hand and released a blazing stream of purple light like fireworks. It faded almost immediately into a fine mist from which a turtle took shape before it dissolved into nothing. "Healing." Her other hand moved to release a red light that became a badger. "Sight." A green raven with a glowing silver eye materialized above her. "Strength." The next burst of light was blue and morphed into a snarling wolf's head. In the moment when the image might have released a low growl of its own, the old woman's white eyes flickered toward Lily and Romeo for only a second. They glanced at each other, and Romeo slipped his hand into hers.

"We have magic, yes. The ability to create." The old woman hunched again and lowered her hands to the pebbly beach. She looked like she attempted to lift a boulder ten times her own weight but a green shoot sprouted from the dry, barren soil. It grew almost instantly into a small tree two feet taller than the storyteller witch, its branches heavy with leaves and budding flowers. "To destroy." The woman swept her arm across in front of her as if slapping someone with the back of her hand. An earsplitting crack erupted from the newly grown tree, which fell into a perfect arrangement of dry, aged wood no one could have positioned any better if they'd spent an hour in the attempt. "Sometimes both." When the woman clapped her hands, the logs that had just been a tree erupted into flame. The force of it ruffled the storyteller's long, yellow-white hair and spread to lift the drummers' hair away from their faces where they knelt.

The warmth of it tickled Lily's cheeks and neck. Romeo sucked a breath in through his teeth.

"My clan and I have come to restore the flames of story in your hearts tonight. To strengthen every bond of magic within your circle. To bring to life the thing that powers us and unites us. And magic, in turn, will always respond. We are the keepers of magic's force, and tonight, we offer you a taste of the source itself. Join us." The old woman spun in a quick circle on light, nimble feet and gestured to every witch—and the one werewolf among them.

Her drummers leapt to their feet and began a new beat together. It was much softer and slower this time, myste-rious and hinting at what was to come instead of the boisterous announcements they'd made this far. Moving in perfect oneness, all five musicians took slow, steady steps away from the old storyteller, hunched over their drums, and each played their own rhythm that mingled with the others into a complicated pattern impossible to replicate. The storyteller lowered her hands to her sides and released a slow, controlled breath like waves crashing on an ocean shore. Her face was raised to the sky black with night now, and shadows played over her face from the roaring fire she'd summoned and the flickering candle flames overhead.

"Okay," Romeo whispered. "I'm officially impressed."

"It's kinda hard not to be." Lily squeezed his hand. "It looks like it's time to get comfortable." She nodded toward the other witches in the circle, who were all in the process of hunkering down to find the right place to sit on the rocks, pebbles, and sand that would provide a good view. She and Romeo lowered themselves onto the dry, uneven ground. "We shoulda brought a blanket or something," she muttered.

"How 'bout this?" He crossed his legs and spread his arms in invitation.

She pursed her lips in fake consideration and shrugged with a tiny smile. "I guess that works." Without further delay, she settled herself in his lap between his crossed legs and grinned when he wrapped his arms around her and rested his chin on her shoulder.

There was a small rise in the level of the other witches' hushed voices around them, punctuated by the storyteller's massive bonfire crackling and shooting sparks onto the beach. But all other sounds died down quickly enough.

The ancient storyteller drew in another long, slow, hushing breath before she began.

"Our lives in this world move on a spinning wheel, subject to time. They are moved by the will of age and experience and of memory and longing. But before time made himself known to us in this existence, there was only magic and dream."

EIGHT

The story was, in and of itself, magical enough. The storyteller moved with every word to shuffle around the circle of gathered witches—not because she couldn't move any faster but because she drew their attention and their eagerness to listen out of each and every one of them. *It's like unraveling a sweater by pulling on a string,* Lily thought. *She's using that string to make something else completely.*

The drummers highlighted the points of their matriarch's story with different beats that followed the volume of her voice. The old woman brought the whole thing to life with even more magical demonstrations—a kaleidoscope of multicolored butterflies, a painting of the entire world in a panoramic view, or some other glittering force around the woman as she spoke. It made Lily's eyes water and her pulse race through her veins.

Romeo swayed a little where they sat, and she frowned over her shoulder at him. "Are you okay?"

He swallowed thickly. "This is..." His eyes were clenched tightly shut, although he couldn't help but smile. "This is way more intense than Montreal."

"I bet." She giggled and hushed herself hastily. "I feel it too, actually. I think we're getting drunk off pure magic. Should—" A golden light flashed through the entire circle of witches and the storyteller's voice lowered into a dark, deep tone of intoxicating mystery. "Do you wanna go?"

He shook his head and opened one unfocused eye to look at her. "Not...yet." His arms tightened briefly around her waist before they slackened again.

"Lemme know when you do."

"...so all would know his name!" The storyteller thrust her arms upward again and her drummers pounded so rapidly on their drums that it sounded like one continuous roar. In the next moment, all the light around them disappeared completely—there were no stars, no candles, and no bonfire, only pure black. A few gasps and murmurs of awe rose from the gathered witches. The old woman's face illuminated once more in the complete darkness, and the flickering flames of her bonfire slithered slowly back into light and focus.

Romeo sucked in a breath and sneezed three times in quick succession, which almost knocked her out of his lap. The narrator uttered a piercing cackle, and a few other witches chuckled. The flames returned to the candles, the stars reappeared overhead, and they could see more than only the old woman's face again.

The powerful witch beside the bonfire exhaled a long, satisfied sigh. "You honor us, dear one."

"Romeo," Lily whispered and gave his arms around her a little shake.

"Huh?"

She couldn't stop staring at the woman, whose blind white eyes—now reflecting the orange glow of the fire—focused intently on Romeo. "I think she's talking to you."

"To—" He sneezed again and burst out laughing.

"That is the joy of being among us," the old woman said and raised her voice again. "Let us be that joy tonight." When her surprisingly straight posture sagged again into the hunch of an old crone, the drummers rose from where they'd sat around her and finally lowered the drums at their sides. They grinned at each other, and the circle of witches who'd seen the most intensely magical show of their lives burst into cheers and applause. The storyteller laughed with them, and the party resumed. Only this time, they'd all received a dose of magic in its rawest form from the keepers of magic themselves. It didn't impact any of them nearly as hard as it did Romeo.

"This is insane," he muttered.

She slid off his lap and frowned at him in concern. "Are you all right?"

"Never better." His heavy eyelids opened slowly beneath his raised eyebrows, and his gaze drifted constantly away from her face. Shaking his head, he blinked and finally managed to focus on her. "God, you're beautiful."

A fit of giggling overwhelmed her, and suddenly, they both laughed so hard it brought tears to their eyes. She threw her arms around his neck and pressed her mouth against his. The force of it thrust him onto his back and he pulled her down with him. "What are we doing?" she whispered, sprawled on top of him.

"Whatever we want." A lazy grin spread over his face.

"At a party. With storyteller magic and so many other witches." She grinned at him, then kissed him again as his hands slid down her back before they settled on her hips. After a deep breath, she jerked away from him and spluttered. "Oh, my God. We're...everyone's...what are we doing?" She rolled off him and sat quickly, swiping her mussed hair back from her forehead as she dragged in another ragged breath. "Woah."

"It's my turn to ask if you're okay, I think." Grunting, he pushed himself up to sit beside her and sighed. "I think it's starting to wear off a little."

"Yeah, no kidding." She tucked her hair behind her ears and looked at him. "We could've actually— I mean—"

He laughed. "We could've. Not that I don't want to. But it's probably not a good idea right here in front of everyone."

"Ya think?" She snorted and shook her head vehemently. None of the other witches paid them any attention and they all seemed to need to recover from the overwhelming intensity of experiencing magic and story together from the source. Everyone milled around now with wide smiles, talking and laughing, and some began to dance to the light tune of a fiddle playing somewhere. "I don't even see a fiddle."

"What?"

"Oh. It's...more magical music, I think. Come on." Lily straightened her shirt, rose slowly to her feet, and stuck her hand out.

Romeo took it and definitely needed her help to stand. He stumbled somewhat and shook his head. "I'll be fine."

"I know."

"Children." The storyteller stepped slowly toward them, the hunch in her upper back impossible to ignore. She'd shed her aged appearance during her performance, but that didn't change the fact that she was still an old woman. Despite her blindness, no one accompanied her toward the friends, who stared with wide eyes and had no idea what to say. "I am a lucky witch tonight," she said, grinning to reveal her toothless gums. "I have seen two separate worlds collide into one. Quite literally, eh?" She uttered another squawking cackle and sniffed a few times. "You two bring a bridge of harmony to what has been broken among us. I would like to honor it." Her wrinkled, crooked hand raised toward Romeo's face and paused.

He glanced at Lily in surprise and enough apprehension that she would have laughed if they hadn't been standing in front of such a powerful witch. Instead, she merely nodded.

"Um...okay." He shrugged.

"Thank you." The blind woman who could still somehow see what she needed to see raised her hand to his face and traced smooth, gentle lines across his brow, cheekbones, and the bridge of his nose. "Oh, yes. It is good you are here." He giggled like she was tickling his armpits instead. When she removed her hand, he stared at her in bemusement. Lily flinched when the storyteller's hand whipped toward her face and hovered there. "And you?" the woman asked.

"Okay." She pressed her lips together and held the gaze boring into her own. The woman's hand was incredibly soft and quite warm as it trailed the same lines over her face.

"Yes. The both of you. Welcome." She drew her hand away and set it against her heart. "My name is Amal."

"Lily."

"Romeo."

"Yes. Yes. Have either of you ever taken a spirit walk?"

They exchanged a baffled glance. "I don't think so," Lily said.

"You will tonight. You'd better find another drink." The woman's next shriek of laughter sounded more like a choke. "Then join us. Perhaps you will find what you're looking for, hmm?" She turned and shuffled away from them, calling out someone else's name and waving her hand toward the witch who answered her call.

"Why does everyone keep saying that?" Lily muttered.

"Maybe it's true." Romeo shrugged. "I assume you don't know what a spirit walk is."

"I haven't a clue."

"Well, I don't feel even a little tired. We can stay, or if you wanna go back and—"

"Oh, I'm gonna find out what a spirit walk is." She grinned at him and nodded. "So are you."

"Anything you want, Lil." He still looked a little startled, like he wasn't quite sure yet what had happened. "You know, I have a feeling that it's important to do what that old lady says, but I really don't even wanna touch another beer tonight."

"I'm right there with you."

NINE

They did find bottled water stashed under the canned drinks in one of the coolers. "Oh, man." Lily wiped her mouth and screwed the lid back onto her bottle. "I forgot how hot it still is."

"I basically forgot everything." Romeo lifted his water in a salute. "I feel better now, though."

"Me too. That was something else."

"I wonder how the spirit walk's gonna compare."

They wandered around on the beach for a while longer, exchanging small talk with a group of strangers who seemed way too excited to see them there. "I don't know if it's even gonna happen. People are already starting to leave."

"Maybe they've been cut off." He snorted at the weak joke.

"Yeah, that's it, I'm sure."

Over half of the original group of witches had strolled away to leave something like fifteen of them in the firelight on the beach, plus the old-crone storyteller and her drummers. Suzanne and Fred ended a conversation with a much smaller group of witches and moved toward the young couple again.

"What do you think?" Suzanne asked, her high voice incredibly loud now that she wasn't trying to be heard over so many other voices. "I do hope you two have enjoyed yourselves."

"Well, I've never seen a storyteller in person before tonight," Lily said. "So that's been incredible. Thank you."

"Oh, this was your first?" She punctuated the question with a piercing giggle. "You sweet thing. That's even better! You know, I am so glad you two—"

A loud thump from the drummers again brought the woman to a complete stop. The remaining witches turned toward the sound, and Amal shuffled across the beach again toward the bonfire she'd created. "Journey with me," she said and gestured toward the fire as she spoke to no one in particular.

"Will this be your first spirit walk as well?" Suzanne asked and stared at them again with wide eyes.

"Yep."

"Oh. Fantastic!" The woman almost bounded away toward the fire as everyone else slowly made their way there too.

Her husband Frank stayed behind to watch her but turned toward Lily and Romeo again and shrugged. "This was the hardest part for me to come to terms with," he said in a low, gruff voice. "Magic was simple, you understand? I saw it with my own eyes, and that was that. A spirit walk?

Well, I merely assumed it only held as much stock as you put into it. Right up there with crystal balls and palm readings and that woo-woo crap." He nodded toward the gathering circle around the bonfire. "I'm sure there are still a few folks out there who like to pretend they can do what that woman does. As a complete human who married into this world, I can tell you this is the real deal. It's definitely worth a shot if you have any questions you need answering." He nodded at them again with a tiny smile lifting the corners of his mouth before he went to join his wife.

"A non-magical trying to convince us that magic is real," Lily muttered. "I've never seen that before."

Romeo nodded. "I like Frank."

She glanced at him and patted his chest. "Of course you do."

"What's that supposed to mean?"

"He's a little rough around the edges, and he's quiet."

"Huh." He tried to look like he hadn't already considered these things but didn't quite manage it.

She chuckled and caught his hand to half-drag him with her toward the fire and the much smaller circle of witches now seated around it. The five drummers had also joined the circle rather than take their places in the center and their drums rested quietly behind them. The storyteller hunched over her crossed legs beside them, no longer the central focus but commanding as much attention. It was a far more intimate setting this time.

"We might have to keep our comments to ourselves," Lily whispered as they approached the last two open places in the circle. "I don't think we'll get away with not being heard."

"Being heard is the intention, tonight," Amal said. Lily started, and Romeo chuckled before they both lowered themselves onto the pebbly beach and crossed their legs. The woman's colorless eyes stared into the fire. "Of course, we all want to be heard. Acknowledged and recognized for who we are, yes? We are not the only ones. The spirits also wish to be heard. They are our ancestors and our guides, forces beyond our everyday awareness that we may or may not know are with us while we travel our own personal paths. A spirit walk brings us together to listen and to be heard—living persons embodying what magic has provided and spiritual beings composed of what magic has always been. Let us walk together now, hmm?"

Lily settled her hands in her lap and watched the other witches around the fire. Most of them stared into the flames. A few focused on the old woman's wrinkled face that flickered with shadows. Some had closed their eyes. When she looked at Romeo, she found him watching her. She widened her eyes at him and waited for what came next.

"Does anyone here wish to receive what they are meant to hear tonight?"

"I do, storyteller." A man with a long, graying ponytail raised his chin toward Amal and nodded.

"Ah. Very good." She nodded but did not look away from the fire. "What is your name?"

"Ken."

The old woman took a deep breath, rested her elbows

on her bent knees, and spread her hands. "We come to walk with our brother Ken and receive his message." The beach fell completely silent for a few minutes. In the quiet, a log in the fire snapped and hurled a spray of sparks that spiraled into the dark sky. A gust of wind that didn't touch anyone else rippled through Amal's yellow-white hair, lifted it away from her face, and blew it over her shoulders in a long, billowing trail. The wind settled, and the old woman smiled. "Your sister Trisha is here with us, Ken."

The man puffed out a huge breath and his shoulders sagged with both mourning and relief.

"She knows that if she were still alive, you would ask her advice about selling the shop." Amal's white eyes reflected the glowing fire and she did not look away. "She is telling you now to sell it anyway. Take the money and go to Boca Raton."

The man burst into laughter and slapped his knee, although tears glistened on his cheeks. "I can't say no to that." A few of the other witches chuckled. "It was our plan, anyway."

"It is still your plan." The old woman nodded.

"Thank you."

She tilted her head, her gaze locked on the fire. "Without your willingness to listen, I am nothing. Do not thank me unless you also thank yourself." She lowered her head incredibly slowly as if she might be drifting off to sleep. "Who else wishes to listen?"

"I do." A tiny, middle-aged woman with short, spiky hair and wearing a neon-pink sweater smiled at the storyteller.

"Ah." Amal's head whipped up again, and one of her hands jerked up. "I do not need to know your name, sister. Your teacher has waited a long time to come forward. And now, you are ready." The woman sucked in a huge, gasping breath, then raised her face to the sky and exhaled. A golden stream of light burst from her open mouth and coalesced into the shape of a lizard that floated above the fire. "The horny toad has been with you," she said. "He is pleased with the work you're doing with your family's reliquary. He also wishes you to know that you do not need help from either your professional peers or your grandson. Continue your work as you always have. And..." She coughed slightly. "Cactus water will help you connect with him on your own whenever you seek more guidance."

The orange lizard flashed, then darted toward the woman in the neon-pink shirt and into her chest. The woman uttered a small, startled squeak, then focused on the fire with wide eyes. "Oh."

"Yes, it has always been there. It is surprising when we finally see it, eh?" Amal cackled, then fell quiet once more.

"Storyteller?" Suzanne leaned forward where she sat beside her husband.

"Hmm?"

The woman glanced at Lily, nodded, and grinned. "Lily is a guest tonight. She told me she's never walked this path before. I wonder if—"

The ancient witch barked out a laugh. "Yes, my dear. I see this too. Our sister must be willing to be still and receive."

Lily blinked. "I'm sorry?" Amal said nothing more, but

Suzanne nodded furiously and showed the younger woman two thumbs-up. "Oh, no. I'm not trying to communicate with anyone's spirit. Really."

"But you do have questions, do you not?" For the first time during the spirit walk, the storyteller removed her gaze from the fire to focus unseeing eyes on her.

"Um..." She glanced at Romeo, who tried to hide a smile and shrugged.

"It's your call."

"I guess there are a few things I'd like to know."

"Isn't that the trick of it?" Amal asked with another laugh. "We would like to know and yet we close the doors to knowing. Sister, are you ready to receive the knowledge you seek?"

She bit her lip. *How can she know anything about my mom?* "Yes."

"Beautiful." The storyteller lowered her chin to her chest again, and everyone waited in silence. The seconds stretched on until a faint snore rose from the old woman. The other witches seemed as confused as Lily, and Romeo only shrugged when she glanced at him.

She leaned toward him and whispered, "Do you think—"

"There are no spirits come to share with you tonight." Amal's voice seemed to rustle in the night air as a low croak. "You travel with the only guide you need. Nothing wishes to be shared."

"Um, well..." She cleared her throat. "I wasn't really expecting—"

"But there is...something..." Amal shook her head,

which was still lowered almost all the way forward against her chest. "Looking for you, sister. Something searching this wide world to find you."

She licked her lips when her stomach curdled at the reminder of whatever witches had tried to kill her at home in Charleston. Her friend grasped her hand.

"I cannot reveal the type of message before I channel it through myself, Lily." The storyteller raised her head and turned blind eyes on the young witch one more time. "Do you wish me to deliver what I feel is there?"

Romeo leaned toward her and whispered in her ear, "You don't have to keep doing this."

She looked at him. "If it helps at all, it's stupid to say no," she pointed out and turned toward the other witch. "Yes, storyteller. I want to know."

"Yes..." Amal pressed her palms together in front of her chest and took a deep breath. "It comes..." The woman huffed out a short breath, then another, and she did not stop until her chest heaved with choppy pants. *She sounds like she's gonna throw up a hairball,* Lily thought. The storyteller rocked where she sat, her breathing ragged and her head thrown back to face the starry sky. A coarse, wordless shout erupted from her mouth, and the logs in the fire all split in half as one to pinwheel sparks and smoke.

It wasn't normal fire smoke, however. This was black and thick and churned out of the flames in a roiling, billowing cloud. It twisted over and over on itself, climbed higher, and spread over the fire toward every witch seated in the circle. The old woman's shout echoed from the shadowy mass itself as if some other person were inside the blackness, fighting to get out. The cloud exploded and a huge black bird emerged from its center. The firelight made it seem that it too was burning. Thick, massive wings spread with a gust of air over the gathered witches with a rumbling growl over the entire beach. The fire snapped again, and the entire column of smoke, bird and all, was sucked into the flames and the logs—maybe even the pebbles beneath—until all of it was gone.

Only then did Lily realize how hard she was squeezing Romeo's hand. And how hard he squeezed hers in return.

TEN

The gathering fell completely silent and the night itself seemed to hold its breath. Lily glanced at Suzanne and felt even worse at the sight of the woman staring at her in absolute terror rather than excitement.

Amal cleared her throat. "I'm sorry." Her blind eyes flickered to the fire, and she turned her head to survey the gathered witches with whatever sight her magic allowed. Even her drummers looked like they'd seen someone die. The woman licked her lips. "That...that I could not see. Did anyone else?"

"It was a bird," Lily said, and she had to clear her own throat to speak louder. "In a black cloud."

"Which type of bird?"

She glanced at Romeo again, and he nodded slowly. "A heron."

The storyteller hissed through her teeth. "The heron carries patience and determination. But—" She tilted her head and frowned before she leaned forward over her crossed legs with a sudden pain in her stomach. "I do not think it is for you, sister."

Lily took a deep breath to calm her rapid heartbeat and nodded. "Thanks, anyway." *I knew this was a bad idea.*

"No need." Amal grunted. "I think...I think I'm finished for the night. I had hoped to—" She shook her head. "Thank you all for being here. We may meet again to finish this tomorrow night, but for now, I..." She closed her eyes and stretched a hand toward the drummer seated beside her. Her aged fingers crawled up his crossed leg, and the man took it in both of his own. "Yes. I am finished." The drummer stood, and two others came to help him lift the storyteller to her feet. She groaned and let them lead her away, showing for the first time that night how much her aging body was already failing her.

In the silence, the other witches rose one after another from the circle. None of them looked at Lily except for Suzanne. "Why do I get the feeling I crashed the party?" she muttered.

Romeo shook his head. "You didn't do anything wrong." He pushed quickly to his feet and offered her a hand to help her up.

Suzanne mumbled a few parting words to the witches who stood beside her and Frank and nodded at them with a tight-lipped smile. When everyone else had wandered away, the older couple approached the young witch and the werewolf.

"I'm so sorry," Lily said, her gaze on the others who walked away.

The woman shook her head and put a gentle hand on

Lily's shoulder. "Don't apologize. For anything. These things..." She looked over her shoulder at the last of the party making their way up the trail toward the campsite. "This happens sometimes. It's no one's fault. I think...well, if Amal were younger, she would have tried again to get you a more specific answer. It's hard to be reminded of how old the woman really is—that she has her own physical limits too, you know?"

"Yeah. She really didn't seem to have any until it was my turn."

"I owe you an apology, Lily." She released the younger woman's arm and placed her hand over her heart. "I didn't in any way mean to push you, and I realize it would have been better if I'd let you come to your willingness on your own. I've learned that when we're not ready for something, there's usually a good reason to hold ourselves back. And I do hope this hasn't left a sour taste in your mouth for the spirit walks. They're usually not that...intense."

"At least not that kind of intensity," Frank added.

"I believe you," she said. "I guess it simply wasn't the right night for me to get my answers."

Suzanne tilted her head and offered her a sympathetic smile. "You'll get them eventually. You'll see." She gazed at her for an uncomfortably long time before she pasted a grin onto her face. "Well. I suppose we're all calling it a night, then. How long are you two staying?"

"Only the one night," Romeo said and put his arm around Lily again. "We still have a long way to go tomorrow."

"Of course. Well, it was very nice to meet you two.

Take care of each other, hmm? And I hope our paths cross again someday."

"Goodnight." Lily waved gently. Frank looked at each of them in turn, nodded, and followed his wife up the path. When they disappeared around the bend at the top of the shallow rise, she sighed. "I don't know if all this hospitality is making me feel better or worse."

"Hey, you gotta know none of that was your fault."

She looked at Romeo and frowned. "It feels like it, though. You saw that black cloud."

"Yep. It looked exactly like the one you unleashed in the speakeasy."

"Only this time, it had a black heron in it—like the business card and the club owner's office. The storyteller said something was looking for me. These things are obviously connected."

Romeo held her closer and they headed up the path toward the campsite. "You know, if I hadn't seen how powerful that woman was, I'd simply tell you not to believe anything she said or pay any attention to what happened."

"But you know it was real too, don't you?"

"Well, yeah. That black cloud and the heron don't show up for everybody. And most people aren't being searched for by something that won't show up as a spirit she could've channeled like she did for the others. Plus, the woman's blind. I know it sounds weird, but I could've sworn she could actually see—that both of those things were real at the same time."

"I think that's part of her magic." With her arm around his waist, she leaned her head against his chest.

"I know. But she couldn't even see any of the stuff she coughed over the fire trying to find your message. That part creeped me out."

"That's why I feel like I ruined everybody's night."

He jostled her shoulder and she finally had to laugh. "Nobody ruined anything, Lil. Nobody was hurt. People weren't pissed off, only weirded out. And we'll be gone in the morning."

She looked at him and took a deep breath. "You really don't feel bad about ending the party they invited us to?"

He shrugged. "Sure, I feel a little bad. I already make witches nervous enough when I'm around anyway. But I know the difference between caring about people and worrying about something I won't ever be able to change. Quit beatin' yourself up, okay?"

"Okay." They stepped across the dry, brown dirt of the campsite, which was mostly dark now that almost everyone in the RVs or various tents had turned in for the night. As they approached the Winnie, she frowned in thought. "You know, there's still one good thing that came out of the whole spirit walk disaster."

"Oh, yeah?" With a gentle smile, he opened the Winnebago's side door.

"Yeah. The storyteller said there weren't any spirits looking for me. You know, dead people wanting to get in touch and tell me whatever important thing they had to say." She looked at him and grinned. "Not even my mom."

He squinted at her for a moment before his eyes grew wide. "Oh."

"If I wasn't already convinced that she's not dead, I

would be now. Storytellers are more connected to magic than any other kind of witch. I'd almost call it proof that she's still alive."

Romeo nodded and held the door open for her while she stepped into the RV and switched on the lights. "How many other people do you think are gonna believe the same thing?"

"Definitely not a court if I want to prove her will was fake and get her declaration of death revoked, or whatever they call it."

"But no one's gonna say you're still overwhelmed by grief when you bring her with you, huh?"

She grinned at him and kicked her shoes off. "We merely have to find her first."

ELEVEN

Lily stirred reluctantly and groaned at the morning sunlight streaming through the bedroom window and directly across her face. "We shoulda closed the curtains."

"Go find the shovel," Romeo grumbled.

"What?"

He rolled toward her and frowned with his eyes still closed until she couldn't help but laugh. His eyes opened at the sound and he peered around him, his face puzzled. "Woah—oh..." Lily laughed again. "That was one of the weirdest dreams I've ever had."

"Oh, that was a dream, huh?" She stretched under the covers and snuggled into him. "I thought that was your weird way of telling me to go take care of it myself."

"Huh?"

"You told me to go find the shovel."

He smirked and tried to look unconcerned. "Weird

dream and talking in my sleep. Awesome." He wrapped his arms around her, toyed with the hem of the tank top she'd changed into before bed, and chuckled.

"What?"

"Nothing."

"Oh, come on. What's so funny?"

He looked at her and tugged on her shirt. "The day we left on this trip, you said you sleep naked. I haven't seen it since then."

"You—" She snorted. "I sleep naked when I'm alone. How 'bout that?"

"Doesn't that seem a little backward to you?" She pinched the skin on his chest, which only made him laugh again. "Hey, I'm merely waiting for you to slip back into your old habits. That's all."

Lily scoffed and sat up to tuck her hair behind her ears. "Forget old habits. It's nothing but new ones since we started this trip." She glanced at him and grinned.

"The two don't have to be mutually exclusive."

"Maybe they won't be. Eventually." She made a face at him and scrambled out of bed in her tank top and pajama shorts. "I'm hungry. Do you want breakfast?"

Romeo stretched his arms above his head and growled. She stared at his bare chest and waited for him to say something. "I always want food."

"Okay. Great. I'll go find something to eat." Smirking, he rolled over and fluffed the pillow under his head. She rolled her eyes and stepped out into the kitchen. With the cabinets open, she scanned what little they'd bought to stock the Winnie and called, "All right. It looks like bagels or—"

She paused at a sharp rap at the RVs side door.

"Is someone knocking?"

"Yep. I got it." Her gaze narrowed. Whoever it was stood really close to the front door and the shadow of their head shifted a little against the sunlight through the small window. She walked down the two steps to the door and pushed it open slowly, ready for whoever it was with a defense spell to be used. The person outside the door jumped back with an exclamation of surprise before Suzanne laughed.

"Oh, good morning," the woman said, tossing her head with a broad grin.

"'Morning," Lily said.

"I just...well." She sighed. "I didn't think you two would still be here this late in the morning, so I wanted to come say hello."

"This late—what time is it?" She blinked against the sun and the heat already evident in the desert.

"A little after eight."

Trying not to laugh, she pressed her lips together and nodded. "I guess we needed a little more sleep than normal."

"Well, that's good. I'm glad you got what you needed. I..." She lifted a small wicker basket lined with a red-and-white-checkered cloth. "I baked bran muffins for our trip out here, and you know, we have many extras. So...would you like some muffins?" The woman shoved the basket almost into her face, but she took the offering with her free hand and smiled.

"Um, thank you. That's really nice of you."

"I warmed them a little for you." Suzanne glanced around nervously, then offered another tight smile. "I honestly feel awful. About last night."

"Oh, no. Please don't. It's—"

"Still. The closest I get to magic is in the kitchen, so I wanted to bring you these. And we'd love to see you off whenever you're ready to pack up and head out of here."

"Okay."

"When are you leaving?"

Lily's mouth popped open. "Well, we just woke up."

"Oh, right. Right. Not a problem. I'll, uh... I'll let you get back to your morning."

"Okay."

Suzanne seemed completely unsure whether she wanted to remain there for chitchat or if she wanted to run away at full speed. She finally settled for something in the middle and walked away hesitantly but turned once to look at the young woman and open her mouth before she closed it again and hurried off.

"Weird..." Lily whispered. But the bran muffins tucked under the checkered cloth smelled amazing, so she closed the Winnie's door behind her and stepped inside.

"Was it that Suzanne lady?" Romeo asked from the bedroom doorway as he scratching his head vigorously.

"Yep." She stared at the basket, then set it on the counter. "She brought us muffins."

"Sweet." He almost ran into the kitchen as she

unfolded the edges of the cloth. "Man, those smell good." His first bite took half the muffin, and he turned to take the milk from the fridge. "What kind are they?"

"Bran muffins. Can you get the butter out too?"

"Like bran cereal?" He set down two glasses, filled them, and slid the butter toward her across the counter. A knife clattered after it.

"I think so, yeah." She eyed him as she sliced her first muffin. Romeo was already reaching for his second while he drained half the glass of milk in one breath. "You might wanna take it easy on those, though."

"Are you kidding? They're still warm. That's the best time to not to be easy on anything." His second muffin disappeared quickly and he stretched for a third.

"Seriously." Lily snorted and pressed her lips together. "Don't eat them all at—"

"I see what you're doing, Lil." He squinted and waved the half-eaten muffin at her. "You want more for yourself."

"Well, yeah. But not all of them in one sitting. You're really gonna feel—"

"Hey, when you said nothing but new habits on this trip, that only applied to you. I'm gonna keep my old ones up and eat my half of these muffins however I want. They're incredible." He stared with wide eyes at the last of it in his hand.

Lily buttered her first and shook her head. "You really can't compare me sleeping naked to what those muffins are gonna do to you."

"What, you mean make me full and happy?"

She looked up at him and winked. "Don't say I didn't warn you."

For a few seconds, he studied her with a raised eyebrow, frowned slightly, and looked at the muffin before swallowing. "Naw. I'm calling your bluff, Lil."

"Okay." Her first bite made her roll her eyes. "They are so much better with butter."

"They're perfect on their own." He wiggled his eyebrows, ate the last of his, and drained the rest of his milk. "It's time to get dressed."

He stalked off toward the bedroom and she ate as slowly as possible to enjoy the muffin and give herself time to grow full. Romeo opened the wardrobe doors across from the bed and retrieved his clothes, which had been in his trekking backpack when they started this trip. "Does that count as moving in with me?"

"What's up?" he asked and leaned back to catch her eye through the doorway.

"Nothing." She crammed the rest of the muffin into her mouth, drank the much smaller glass of milk he'd poured for her, and stuck the few dishes they'd used into the dishwasher. "I'm definitely saving the muffins for later."

***

"ARE you sure you don't wanna hang around for a little longer?" Romeo asked as they stepped out of the Winnie to disconnect from the electrical hookups. "We only have five hours of driving today. We can totally take our time."

"Romeo." Lily lowered her voice and glanced around the campsite. Every person outside at Santa Rosa Lake was another witch she recognized from the night before. "There's not really anything to do here. It's already way too hot and there's no shade, and I have a feeling everyone's waiting for me to ruin their next spirit walk."

He bent to disconnect the extension cords and didn't look at her when he responded. "I thought you weren't gonna keep beating yourself up about that."

"I'm working on it. Hey, if there's anything cool around here that has air-conditioning and doesn't include being roasted in a desert oven, I'm all for it."

"Yeah, I think we can find something like that."

"Well, so far, your travel-planning abilities haven't steered us wrong."

He straightened and nodded in agreement. "Yes. They haven't, have they?" Grinning, he looped the cables quickly. "I'd say I'm fairly good at getting us where we need to go."

"Absolutely." She turned to scan the other parked RVs again. "Hey, I'm gonna go give this to Suzanne. She wanted us to say goodbye before we leave."

"Yeah, sure. I'll be right there."

With the woman's gift basket grasped with both hands, Lily headed toward the retro Airstream a few sites down, where Suzanne had set the picnic table up beside it with the full shebang—tablecloth, place settings for two, an iced pitcher of tea, and a vase with flowers. "Those have to be fake, right?" The woman looked up from where she set the last piece of silverware in place and Lily grinned. "Good morning. Again."

This time, Suzanne's smile seemed far less forced. "Lily. Hello." She wiped her hands on her capris and shrugged. "I'm getting ready for our own breakfast. We like to eat a little later."

"Well, thanks to you, we didn't have to make breakfast at all. I wanted to get this basket to you before we headed out. The muffins were excellent."

"Oh, how sweet. Thank you." She took the empty basket and set it on the picnic table. "I'm glad you enjoyed them."

"Romeo might have gone a little overboard, they were that good." Lily glanced over her shoulder to see him heading toward them. "He had three."

The other woman's eyes widened. "Oh, he—three?"

She tried not to laugh. "Yeah."

Suzanne lowered her head and leaned toward her. "Has he had them before?"

"I don't think so."

The Airstream door opened, and Frank stepped out as Romeo joined them. "Morning," the man said. "Are you folks heading out now?"

"That's the plan." Romeo stepped forward to shake his hand, and the man nodded curtly. "We had a great time last night. Thanks for inviting us. And those muffins—"

"I heard you had three." The woman pressed her lips together against a smile.

"At least." He chuckled. "I couldn't stop. That's always a good sign."

"Maybe not," Frank muttered. Suzanne uttered a playful gasp and smacked the back of a hand against her husband's arm. "Have you ever had bran muffins before?"

"Not until today. I think I might have to make them a regular thing."

The older man laughed for the first time and shook his head. "Regular's definitely the right word, son." His wife rolled her eyes.

Romeo laughed with the man but his smile faltered. "I think I missed the joke."

"You'll get the punchline soon enough." Frank slapped his arm.

"Frank, you're awful," Suzanne chided.

"What happens with a man and his bran muffins isn't anyone else's business," he replied.

Lily had to look away from them to hold her laughter in check. "Well, the rest are for me. I'll be enjoying them over time."

Frank winked at her. "Smart woman."

"But really. Thank you both for everything." She nodded at the older couple. "We got to check a few things off our list of experiences last night. And you've been so welcoming. That was nice."

"Well, witches and their counterparts gotta stick together, right?" Frank smirked. "Especially out on the road. There's community everywhere if you know where to look."

"We're a little better at finding it now," Romeo agreed. "That's for sure."

"You two enjoy the rest of your trip, wherever you're

headed." Suzanne clasped her hands against her heart again and glanced from Lily to Romeo with wide, glistening eyes. "And take care of each other. I said it when you first got here, and I'll say it again. You two have something special. Don't let it go."

Romeo glanced at Lily and smirked. "Yeah. We know." He nodded at the older couple. "Take care."

"Bye." Lily lifted her hand in farewell before they turned and headed across the campsite.

"Seriously, though," he muttered. "What's so funny about the muffins?"

She shrugged. "I'm gonna have to go with Frank on that one. It's nobody's business but yours."

"What does that even mean?"

"Only that...experiential wisdom is more powerful than hearing it from someone else."

"You look like you're about to lose it." He squinted at her and couldn't decide whether to smile or beg her to tell him already.

"I'm trying really hard not to."

"Lily." They turned to see one of the drummers from the night before jogging toward them. The man's long white hair was pulled back into a ponytail today, and his leather sandals sent up little puffs of red-gold dust with every step.

"Hi...uh..."

"Lucas." The man offered her his hand and he shook Romeo's next, but that was simply to be polite. "Amal would like to speak with you before you leave," he told her. "If you're open to a quick chat."

"Oh. Sure. Is she...feeling better this morning?"

He flashed a wide grin, his brown eyes bright within the tanned lines around his eyes. "She is. We all have our limits, even a master storyteller, which is easy enough to forget. Even for her students. Come on." He nodded toward the circle of RV sites, and the friends followed.

TWELVE

They reached two large black RVs parked side by side and slightly distant from the others. The vehicles looked twice as big as Lily's Winnebago, although that was impossible. The other drummers sat in foldable canvas chairs under the awning stretched from the first RV and each nursed a drink while they talked and laughed softly. When they saw the visitors, they all offered wide grins and nods of greeting. One woman said, "Good morning, travelers," in a lighthearted, musical voice.

"Morning," Lily said.

"Beautiful day, huh?" Romeo asked and gestured toward the desert around them.

The drummers laughed. "A little too hot, honestly. But to each his own." The man who'd spoken raised his mug in a toast. "Even if you're into this kinda weather, I'll still invite you to wait in the shade with us."

"Go ahead," Lucas said and nodded toward the two

empty chairs arranged beneath the awning. "I'll be back in a minute." He hurried past the first RV toward the second.

"Okay." Lily glanced at Romeo, who gestured toward the open seats. Once seated with the four other drummers, she felt their curious, amused gazes on her and smiled. "Where are you guys headed?"

"Wherever Amal decides to go next." The second woman who hadn't greeted them before tucked her long white hair behind her ear. "We'll be here until she says it's time to move on."

"To another witch gathering?" Romeo asked.

One of the other men—this one with his hair pulled all the way up into a bun on top of his head—shrugged. "Maybe. Maybe not. Many different people ask us if Amal can see the future and if that's how she knows where to go next and who to lead in her stories."

"Can she?" Lily crossed one leg over the other and leaned back in the chair.

The group shared a few secretive chuckles. "We have no idea. If she can, she keeps that to herself. It's part of what makes her such a great teacher."

"We're still learning," the first woman said, and Lily realized this drummer was the only one among them with blue eyes instead of brown. "We joined Amal's clan when we were kids and learned to drum our stories together and to listen to our teacher together. It took us long enough."

"Only until we learned how to let everything else go." The drummer with the bun raised his mug, and the others laughed again.

"And none of you are related?" Romeo asked.

"You know, most people are too mystified to ask any questions at all," the woman who'd first greeted them said. She leaned forward in her chair and grinned. "I like that you do."

The other woman slapped her clan-mate's arm. "We're definitely not related," she said and turned toward the young couple. "A storyteller is born as what they are to any family, anywhere in the world. And Amal came for each of us."

"Well, I thought last night was incredible," Lily said.

"Even the end?" The man with a bun raised an eyebrow and smirked.

"Ryker..." The woman with blue eyes frowned warningly.

He laughed. "I thought it was incredible."

She stiffened a little but tried to remain composed. *At least* they *found it entertaining.*

"Whatever magic's following you around, Lily," he added, "I've never seen anything like it."

"I have." The firm, commanding voice rose from the back of the RV, and everyone turned. Amal shuffled across the dirt, hunched with age, and her hand rested lightly on Lucas' forearm. "And it was only once. That does not mean that it's the same, hmm?" The drummers gazed at her with both respect and amusement and smiled at their teacher. The old storyteller removed her hand from her guide's arm and navigated through the chairs directly toward Lily.

She stood and stared into the old woman's sightless

eyes. *She's not sightless, though. In reality, she sees more than most people ever will.*

"I realize it must be confusing for you to join me this morning after last night." Amal stopped in front of her and extended both hands. She took them. "Know that I've been through far worse than that, my dear, and the sun greeted me today with a clean canvas." The woman grinned her toothless smile and squeezed her hands with surprising strength. "I spent some time seeking guidance in my dreams, Lily. I cannot tell you what it is you will face, but you'll know it when the time comes. And I've been told to give you this." She pushed Lily's palms together and covered her hands with her own. "When you see only darkness, as I once did, use this gift. It will show you what you were always meant to see."

A cool, smooth weight settled between her hands. The storyteller released her, and she opened her palms slowly like an unfolding book to see a two-inch lapis lazuli resting in her hand. She stared at it in bemusement. "Thank you."

"Thank you, child." With one hand, Amal grasped Lily's wrist and patted the young witch's cheek with the other. "You have reminded me that even I cannot see every mystery before it unfolds. I'd say I got the better end of our gift exchange." The woman cackled, released her, and turned toward her drummers, nodding slowly. "Now, which one of you is it who's hiding my tea this morning?" The woman with the blue eyes pointed at her bolder clan-sister. "Jeanette?"

The woman who'd so enjoyed Romeo's questioning rolled her eyes and sighed. "You didn't even give me a chance," she muttered and glared at the other drummers. Another wave of laughter rose among them as the brown-eyed woman fumbled below her chair to withdraw a large, still-steaming mug. She handed it carefully to her teacher, and Amal turned toward Romeo this time.

"You're in my chair, dear boy."

"Oh." He leapt from the canvas chair and stepped aside. "Sorry."

The ancient storyteller threw her head back for another shriek of joy and shuffled toward him. "You'll spend more than enough time sitting today, I think. And it won't be while you're driving."

Lucas chuckled and simply shrugged when Romeo sent him a questioning glance.

Amal's laughter cut out abruptly, and she jerked her hand out to clutch the young werewolf's wrist tightly. She stared at her mug of tea and said in a low voice, "Do not let them break you."

The witches beneath the RV's awning fell silent and all their smiles faded. He swallowed. "I won't."

She gave his wrist a little shake. "Yes. Good." She released him. "Safe travels to both of you."

"You too," Lily blurted. Lucas nodded with a smile, and Romeo looked like he was choking. "Bye." With the blue stone Amal had magicked into her closed hand grasped tightly, she turned with her friend to head to their RV. "Do you still wanna hang out for a while?" she asked when they were hopefully far enough out of earshot.

"Not really, no." He raised his eyebrows. "That was really weird."

"I think we're gonna have to get used to that from here on out. What was she talking about at the end?"

"What, the 'don't let them break me' part?" She nodded. "I have no clue. I won't be surprised if I have bruises later where she grabbed me. I wasn't thinking about asking more questions."

"I get it." She turned the lapis lazuli a few times before she closed her fist around it. "I have a feeling she wouldn't have told you anyway."

"It was about as cryptic as what she told you, huh?"

"Basically, yeah." She opened the Winnie's side door and climbed inside. "I guess we're gonna have to find the answers to that along with everything else."

THIRTEEN

It was Romeo's turn to drive and after a stop to fill up at the first gas station they found, he took them back to the highway for what should have been a straight drive all the way down I-25 to El Paso. It wasn't.

After an hour on the road, he began to shift uncomfortably in the driver's seat.

"Are you okay?" she asked.

"What? Yeah. But..." He frowned and wouldn't quite look at her. "I'm good."

Five minutes later, he swerved onto the next exit and pulled into another gas station like a madman.

"I remember putting gas in the tank," she said and removed her sunglasses to study his reddening face as he shifted into park and left the engine on. "So what else did you forget?"

"I didn't forget anything. I only need a minute." He threw the driver's door open, leapt out, and slammed it shut behind him.

When he appeared in the passenger-side mirror, she sighed as he jogged around the back of the gas station toward the public restroom. He disappeared around the corner, and she waited. The next time she looked at the clock on the dash, he'd already been gone five minutes.

"I hope he's okay. I should tell him, right? He deserves to—what?" A glistening black Ford F-250 backed into the parking lot with one space between it and the Winnie. She caught only a glimpse of it in the side mirror, but when she looked through the window, the decal on the truck's rear window was as plain as day—a black heron, its wings outstretched, on a white oval background.

Trying not to jump to conclusions, she stared at the truck and waited for any movement from inside the cab. The driver spent an inordinate amount of time simply sitting there with an idling engine, but it finally cut off. Sunlight glinted off the door on the other side of the truck, and a man in a black Stetson with a bolo tie beneath the collar of his gray button-down shirt slid out. He walked slowly toward the back of the truck, opened the tailgate, and reached into the crate he'd strapped down to the bed.

Lily didn't move and held her hand below the window so he wouldn't see the fiery-red sparks that crackled around her fingertips. If this was another witch like the one in the gray suit who'd tried to kill her—which seemed likely with the heron on the guy's truck—she'd be ready. "Obviously, they don't care about magical attacks in public," she muttered.

The man drew a cell phone from his back pocket and put it to his ear. He spoke so quietly that she could only hear the timbre of his voice but no words. She jumped when he thumped the tailgate back into place.

"No, he won't be a problem. I told you I'd take care of it," he shouted. That was loud enough. "Let me do my job." The man snarled at his phone and shoved it back into his pocket. Then, he froze.

Lily turned the sparks at her fingertips up a notch.

The angry man in the black Stetson raised his head until the wide brim of his hat no longer hid his eyes and looked directly into Lily's window. She stared at him and all he did was raise and lower his eyebrows quickly. *That feels like a challenge.* He raised a finger to his lips, slapped the raised tailgate, and stormed across the parking lot toward the gas station. His trajectory, however, didn't seem quite right. He was striding around to the restrooms.

"Romeo—" Lily jerked her seatbelt off and shoved the door open. Her flats slapped against the asphalt as she jogged after the cowboy and tried not to draw any more attention to herself than she actually would when she caught up with him. By the time she reached the back of the gas station, the man had already taken hold of the door handle of the men's room. "No, you don't." She flicked her fingers toward the handle, which flashed white and crackled around his fingers.

With a shout of surprise and pain, he staggered off the walkway and clutched his hand to his chest.

"What the hell?" Romeo's voice yelled from inside the bathroom.

"Sorry!" she called.

The man in the Stetson whirled toward her with wide eyes. "What do you—"

"I wasn't talking to you." She stormed toward him and when he reached toward his back pocket again, she acted before he could accomplish whatever he intended to do. A swipe of her hands and a forceful shove with her next spell knocked his feet out from under him. He landed with a thud on the asphalt and groaned. "You know, my gut's telling me to maim first and ask questions later," she said. "But I'm gonna give you a chance to tell me what I wanna know first."

"What?" The man tried to scramble back like a crab and winced.

"Who sent you?" She summoned another sparking red attack spell, but this time, she didn't hold back. The back of the gas station flared with red light. "I'm tired of being chased and threatened and constantly looking over my shoulder. Now, you're gonna tell me who's looking for me so I can make it stop."

"What is that?" The man's gaze remained fixed on the roiling ball of red energy in her hand, even when his voice cracked.

The bathroom door opened with a squeal, and Romeo stepped out, wiping his hands on a paper towel. The door clicked shut behind him and for a few seconds, no one said a word. "What's going on?" he asked and glanced from her to the grown man sprawled awkwardly on the asphalt.

"Hey, brother, this chick's nuts. I don't even—do you see that thing?" The man pointed at Lily's uncast spell.

"Lily—"

"Go ahead," she told the man. "Do you wanna tell him what you were planning?"

With a huff of surprise, he whipped his head to look from one to the other. "Hey, if you guys have somethin' goin' on in there, that's cool. I was only tryin' to take a piss. I'll go somewhere else."

"Nice try." Lily stepped forward, and the man shouted again.

"Woah, woah. Hey." Romeo stepped quickly toward her and put a hand on her arm. "Maybe take a break on the light show for a minute."

"Romeo, I heard the guy said he'll take care of it." She nodded toward the man who still hadn't found enough courage to get up off his ass yet.

Her friend gave her a hasty, tight shake of his head. "I don't think that applies to us."

"Did Cameron tell you to do this?" the man muttered. "Is that it? You can tell him to go to hell, 'cause he's already fired."

Lily's gaze flickered toward him and only then did she realize how terrified he was. Nobody could fake that. She frowned at Romeo. "But I saw—"

He tried to subtly point at his own nose like he was trying to rub it and shook his head again.

"Really?" she asked. "Nothing?"

"Not even a little."

With a huge sigh, she released her attack spell and the red sparks fizzled out.

Her victim leaned away from her when she crouched

in front of him, but he wasn't able to look away. "I'm really sorry."

"Hey, whatever. Can I...can I use the bathroom?"

She nodded. "Yeah, it's all yours. Gimme a sec." She swept her hand quickly in front of his face and conjured the sparkling blue mist she'd used on the witch in the gray suit who'd tried to blow her to pieces in a parking garage. She made sure this memory spell wasn't even half as strong.

His eyes rolled back in his head and he sneezed.

"Oh, my God." Lily put a hand on his knee. "Sir, are you okay?"

"What?"

"I saw you fall. It looked bad, so I..." She glanced at Romeo. "We wanted to make sure you were all right."

He frowned and licked his lips. "Yeah. I...I think so. I don't even..." He scowled at the asphalt beneath him and gazed at the back of the gas station. "Was I going in or out?"

"It looked like you had to make a pitstop." Romeo stepped toward them and offered the man his hand.

The man took it with a frown and tried to shake off the fact that he didn't remember the last three hours or how he'd gotten this far south on I-25. "Yeah. I still do. Uh, thanks." He nodded at Romeo, then glanced at Lily. "I, uh...sorry about the trouble."

"Don't be," she said and tried to smile. "Take it easy, okay?" She met her friend's gaze and turned to head back toward the Winnie. He stepped beside her, and they didn't say anything else until they were back in their seats with both doors closed.

He grabbed his seatbelt to buckle it but paused halfway and let it slide back. "Let me start by saying I know you wouldn't have gone all vigilante without a good reason. Even if it turned out to be a misunderstanding."

She closed her eyes and shook her head. "That's his truck."

"So you saw the heron sticker and assumed he's one of the people after you."

"After us, actually. At least, that's what I thought. It wasn't only the sticker. The guy yelling into his phone and said, 'He won't be a problem' and 'I'll take care of it.'" She shifted in the passenger seat to face him. "Then he looked at me like he knew exactly who I was and headed for the bathroom after you. So, yeah. All the pieces were there and I put them together the way I wanted to see 'em." She spread her arms apologetically. "I'm sorry."

"Well, it's a good thing no one took it any further than that, right?"

With a long sigh, she put a hand to her forehead. "I'm starting to think Mom taught me to be too observant."

"Okay. Wait a minute." Romeo pushed himself out of the driver's seat and sat on the wide center console, one left leg crammed awkwardly against the dash. He pulled her hand down from her face and held it. "First of all, there's no such thing as too observant. You've put together things I would never have been able to see."

"And I still get it wrong." She swallowed around the uncomfortable lump in her throat. "I'm not used to this whole being-on-the-run thing. In secret. While trying to find my mom."

"Good. I'm not used to it either and I don't think we should be. That would really suck." When she looked at him they shared small chuckles of relief. "It's okay to make mistakes, Lil. Otherwise, we wouldn't learn anything."

"Hey, I learned more than enough without making that kinda mistake." She gestured toward her window and the gas station across the parking lot.

"What'd you tell me? Something about experiential knowledge being better than having somebody simply tell you."

"Something like that. But that was about something completely different."

"It doesn't matter." He brought her hand up to his lips, kissed the back of it quickly, and set it in her lap. "You should take your own advice sometimes." With a wink, he slid off the center console and slumped into the driver's seat. A little groan escaped him when he managed to stretch his leg out again under the steering wheel. "And next time, maybe wait for me to come back before going after someone fully Lily Antony style, okay?"

"I thought he was coming after you. In the bathroom."

He shrugged. "Or text me. We have phones."

She raised her eyebrow. "You want me to text you when you're having serious digestive issues?"

His mouth dropped open before he frowned and closed it again. "Okay, so this time was an exception."

"Oh, I know. It's not like you would've been able to drop everything and—" Her own giggle cut her off.

"I'm glad you think it's so funny." He scrunched his face again and rubbed his stomach briefly before he took hold of his seatbelt again. "I don't know what happened, but I almost didn't make it."

Lily's giggle exploded into a shriek of laughter.

"Why is this so hilarious?" He didn't think it was very funny, but the sight of laughing like that always made him laugh.

"You still don't know what happened?" He looked so clueless when he shrugged that she had another good laugh and wiped away the few tears in her eyes. "It's the muffins, Romeo."

"The muffins?"

"Bran muffins."

"Okay, you said they were made of cereal."

She sighed and giggled again. "You know why people eat bran cereal, right?"

He smirked. "I know you're gonna tell me anyway."

"Fiber." She sniffed and wiped her eyes again. He merely stared at her. "You don't... Fiber. Come on. It's—" Another laugh burst out of her but she cut it short. "It's for staying regular."

"Regular with—" His frown exploded into wide-eyed realization. "Oh, shit."

That made her laugh even harder. "Literally," she squealed. "And you ate three of them in five minutes."

"Four, actually." He laughed with her this time and grabbed the gear shift to shove it into reverse but paused. "Okay, why the hell would somebody make muffins outta that stuff? They're delicious!" His eyes were so wide, she thought he might have to go back to the bathroom.

"Are you okay?"

"No. Suzanne was a really nice lady. And that was the cruelest gift ever." A smile broke through his surprise. "You had one too. How come you're not running inside?"

She was laughing so hard now, she couldn't make any sound at all. He glared at her while she hunched over her lap and finally gasped for breath when she literally couldn't go without it any longer. "I eat vegetables," she squeaked.

"Oh, come on." He snorted and shook his head. "That's not why."

She took another deep breath and straightened. "That's totally why. It might be rabbit food, but it builds up an immunity to bran muffins."

For a few seconds, he simply stared at her in genuine disbelief. When her laughter finally died down, his eyes widened. "We should've gotten her recipe, then. I'd eat those things every day. You can keep the salad." Huffing out another almost incredulous breath, he backed the Winnie out of their parking place and turned her to head back onto the highway. "Hey, how much of that guy's memory did you wipe, anyway?"

Lily glanced into the passenger-side mirror at the black Ford. The man in the Stetson walked slowly toward his truck, his cell phone pressed against his ear as he looked around the parking lot in confusion. "Something like three hours. That's about as short a timeline as I've managed."

"How short can they be?"

"Well, a really advanced wipe can erase the last thirty seconds. There are specialists for that, right? Witches who focus all their magic on manipulating memory. I read about one in the fifteenth century who could wipe people's entire lives outta their heads in an instant. Some of the best can even remove specific memories and put new ones in. Or change enough tiny details to make someone's life complete chaos."

"Wow." He made a right turn onto the freeway toward the exit onto I-25. "For the most part, that sounds awful."

"For the most part?"

"Well, it could have positive uses too. Like making me think those muffins tasted like cardboard so I never touched one again."

"Ha." She turned toward him and grinned. "No, I'm sure you had to learn a lesson on that one."

"Oh, yeah? What lesson?"

She shrugged and spread her arms. "Hey, Fred was right. What happens with a man and his bran muffins isn't anyone else's business."

FOURTEEN

They stopped for lunch in a tiny town off the highway that Lily hadn't even paid attention to on the exit signs. She wasn't particularly fond of Cracker Barrel, but Romeo was way too excited about it so she sucked it up and rolled with it.

"Okay, this is the part where we get to take our time a little and simply enjoy ourselves." He held the door open for her as they left the restaurant.

She turned to him and regarded him warily. "Oh, really?"

"Yep. There's this place that's only a slight detour, but it's supposed to be awesome."

"What is it?"

"I don't wanna ruin the surprise." He grinned. "All I can tell you is that it's inside and has AC."

"I love it already."

She made no further effort to pry the surprise out of

him and he flashed her a couple of enquiring glances as they continued as if he wondered why.

They pulled up in front of the Las Cruces Museum of Art a little after 3:00 p.m. "Huh." She stared at the front of the long brown building and the huge blue sign.

"What?"

"Honestly, I didn't expect an art museum."

Romeo turned the engine off and handed her the keys. "Okay, so we made a slight detour. But it was literally down to this or the World's Largest Pistachio Nut. I made an executive decision."

She snorted. "The giant pistachio doesn't have AC, I assume."

"Correct."

The place was surprisingly fairly busy, but it was a Tuesday afternoon in the middle of New Mexico's summer heat. They only had about an hour and a half left before the museum closed, but it was enough time to get out of the Winnie, stretch their legs, and stay out of the ninety-two-degree oven outside.

"It looks like they recently got all new exhibits in," Romeo said and stared at the map he'd collected from the information desk. "If we go down here, we have the Wildlife Highlights and something about...Reality Dreams. I can't even pronounce this woman's name. The other side has something called Robots in the Desert of Disguise and a giant birthday cake made of used napkins. I think."

Lily smiled broadly and tapped the brochure. "My guess is you're leaning toward Wildlife Highlights, yeah?"

"Well, we can go see whatever you want—"

"A cake made of trash doesn't sound too awesome. Let's avoid that part."

"Wildlife it is!" He stuck his elbow out, and she linked her arm through his before they set off. It took them a few minutes to work their way through all the other people who wandered through the displays and around the gift shop. "And here we are." He swept his arm across the next gallery, which was comprised of mostly clay and metal sculptures. "I actually thought there'd be more fur and maybe feathers."

"It's an art museum." She laughed. "It's the nature and science museums that have the stuffed animals."

He shrugged, then gasped and pulled her across the room. "Would you say this fully represents the species as an accurate portrayal?" He spun and positioned his face next to the giant wolf-head sculpture, complete with bared fangs in a silent snarl.

"Are you talking about the statue or yourself?" she asked, raising an eyebrow.

"Hmm. Both?"

"Maybe art curation isn't one of your strong suits."

"Fine."

There was an incredibly impressive collection of turtle shells which had been stacked together to form a giant turtle. "Does it seem a little counterintuitive to use these for a piece dedicated to raising awareness for endangered turtles?" Lily squinted at the plaque beside the sculpture.

"Only one of them's real." Romeo pointed to the line at the bottom.

"Maybe I wasn't cut out to understand the way art works, either." She shrugged.

"Art's simply another kind of magic, right?" He slid his arm around her shoulders and led her to the next row of pieces on display. "I like yours better."

She laughed. "Yeah, me too."

When they reached the far wall of the Wildlife Highlights exhibition, the art in the room had already lost her attention. She was about to suggest they leave when a shadow flickered across the wall and caught her eye, and her gaze fell instantly onto the metal sculpture hung on the wall. Fifty black birds had all been painstakingly attached to each other by the tips of their wings, tailfeathers, the ends of their talons, and a few by their beaks to create the sprawling piece at least four feet in length. "Of course," she muttered.

"What?"

"Of course there are birds. Yeah, I know you're gonna say they're everywhere. But I..." She stopped when she read the title of the artwork—*Everywhere You Go.* "Okay, tell me that isn't weird."

"Not if the artist feels the same way about birds."

She shook her head. "I guess."

He leaned toward her and put his mouth against her ear. "But I did notice something else."

"Oh, real—"

"No, don't turn around." When he gripped her arms a little tighter than normal, she stared blankly at the bird sculpture and forced a smile. "I think he works here. He's been watching us for a while, but he didn't really move until you noticed the birds."

Lily leaned back into Romeo and covered his hand with her own. "Move how?" She turned her head barely enough that he could hear her.

"Toward us. I can smell him. So, at the very least, he could probably take a good guess at what we are."

"Yeah. Two people who paid to get in and enjoy the art museum."

"Honestly, I think it's me."

She turned to face him, wound her arms around his neck, and looked into his eyes. He smiled at her but definitely couldn't hide his discomfort. "You didn't do anything."

"Sometimes, merely being somewhere is enough to cause problems."

"That's not a reason for someone too—"

A huge man in a black button-down shirt and black slacks strolled slowly toward them. Lily glanced briefly at him over Romeo's shoulder. "There's another guy behind you. They look like security."

"Okay." He slid his hands onto her hips and he held her with a little extra pressure. "Whatever they say we need to do, go with it, okay?"

"Romeo, we can't let them—"

"Excuse me, sir." The massive security guard was right behind Romeo now and his chin seemed almost to melt into his thick neck when he spoke.

Romeo looked over his shoulder, then turned halfway and hugged Lily closer. "Hi."

"I need you to come with me, sir." The man beckoned with a choppy wave and nodded.

"Oh, are you guys closing already?" He glanced around and faked looking for a clock. "I didn't think it was four-thirty yet."

The security guard leaned down and lowered his voice even more. "I've been informed that your name's on the museum's blacklist. I'm here to escort you off the premises, which I'd prefer to do with as little force as necessary. No force at all would be ideal."

He looked right into the man's narrow eyes and took a deep breath. "Right. I hear ya loud and clear, man." With a nod, he stepped around the guard and slipped his arm off Lily's shoulders to take her hand instead.

"Blacklist?" she whispered and darted furtive glances over her shoulder. The burly security guard followed closely but still maintained sufficient distance to not make this look like an issue in the museum. "Have you been here before?"

"Nope. I told you. The tall, skinny guy with a mustache was watching us. He knows what I am. I guess that's enough of a reason for him."

"They can't do this." She squeezed his hand.

"Lily, I already know what happens when I try to stand up against it. So, please. Keep walking."

None of the other visitors to the museum paid them much attention on the way out, but another much smaller security guard waited for them at the front doors. This one studied them with his lips pressed together and pushed the door open as they reached it. He held it open for them until they'd stepped outside again. Lily turned before it closed again. The giant folded his arms and stood there, watching them without any emotion whatsoever. She glared at them and shook her head. "This is disgusting."

"Yep. Come on." Romeo hauled her toward the parking lot and the Winnebago, but she caught his arm and tugged him back. He turned and licked his lips, frowning.

"I can fix this." She held his hand in both of hers and nodded.

"Lily—"

"No, really. I can make a call. I know at least three of my mom's co-workers who used to be museum curators. All of them would tell these idiots in a heartbeat that they actually kicked Margaret Antony's daughter out of their establishment and need to make up for it. I can get us back inside."

"They're almost closed, anyway."

"Okay." She scowled and shook her head. "So screw getting into the art museum. The least they can do is apologize to you. You didn't do anything wrong. They have absolutely no right to 'escort us out' based on what they think you are."

"But that's what I am." He pulled his hand out of hers and jerked his head away. "They're not wrong. And I'm really not looking for any handouts, okay?"

"Excuse me?"

"Look, I know that's what you and your mom do. You take on all these charity cases. You help people get back on their feet and that's great. You're probably really good at it."

"Romeo—"

"But I don't need that from you." He frowned at the asphalt in the parking lot, unable to meet her gaze. "I don't need it at all. So can you please gimme the keys? We can forget about the whole thing and keep going."

Lily glanced at the open palm he'd thrust toward her and waited for him to look at her but he didn't. *And he probably won't.* With a deep breath, she retrieved her keys from her purse and dropped them into his hand. He nodded at the ground and walked around the front of the Winnie to climb inside. "I was literally only trying to help," she muttered and scowled at the front doors of the art museum again. She couldn't see anyone through the tinted glass but she waited a little longer before she finally turned her back in case the security guards were still watching them.

When she stepped into the Winnie through the side door, Romeo had already started the engine. His seatbelt was on, both his hands gripped the steering wheel tightly, and he stared directly ahead through the windshield. He still didn't look at her. Lily sat in the passenger seat, buckled her seatbelt, and took a breath. "I really wasn't trying to—"

"I know, Lily." He sighed. "I know. I only need a minute."

"Sure." She bit her lip and stared out the passenger window as he pulled out of the parking lot. Without a word, they headed off for somewhere else that wouldn't kick him out merely for being born as himself.

FIFTEEN

It was only about a forty-five-minute drive until they stopped at the El Paso West Anthony KAO campsite in El Paso, Texas near the Mexican border. Once again, Romeo had somehow found the time when Lily wasn't watching to book a reservation for the night, and they slipped into their designated RV site on the wide, flat, empty expanse of concrete among many more RVs than they'd come across at any of their other locations.

He turned the engine off and left the keys in the ignition when he clambered out to hook them up. She stared through the window at what was basically little more than a parking lot with the foothills of the Franklin Mountains on the western horizon. "So much for relaxing and taking our time." She propped her chin on her fist and watched a woman who had to be in her eighties move slowly down the rows of RVs with a tiny white dog in tow. The animal looked both terrified and exhausted and trembled with every step. *Well, so is the owner. It might only be old age for both of them.* She sighed. "I really should go talk to him."

She unbuckled her seatbelt and crawled across the center console to pull the keys from the ignition. "The last thing we need is to have somebody sneak in to take you for a joyride." They went into her purse and she stepped through the Winnie and out of the side door.

Romeo stood a few feet away, facing the mountains with his hands in his pockets. She closed the door softly behind her and walked toward him, grateful for the few empty sites between them and the other RVs. "Hey."

"Hey." He didn't turn to look at her.

"I'm not gonna bring this up again." She stepped beside him and stopped to stare with him at the mountain range lit up in gold and brown by the early-evening sun. "I only wanna say I'm sorry. I really didn't mean to make it worse."

He took a deep breath, sighed through his nose, and took a few more seconds before he finally looked at her. "You didn't. I've spent my whole life learning how to ignore it. I guess you reminded me that I do actually have a reason to be angry about it. I simply...I don't wanna be pissed off all the time. It feels like the only way to do that is to shove it all under the rug."

"It doesn't have to be the only way." She glanced at him and shrugged.

"Sometimes you just gotta know when to cut your losses, Lily." He looked away again. "I know that's not something you do."

She huffed out a wry chuckle. "Maybe I need to."

"No, you don't. You fight for things because you know they're true and you know what's right. I've always admired that about you. And I envy it a little, I guess. 'Cause I—" He released another sharp, frustrated breath.

"What?"

"The things you stand up for are the things you can prove, right? Like your mom still being out there. Even if people don't believe it, you find a way to show them you were right. Or at least that there's another way to look at things. You've done that since we were kids. Even with me."

"Are you..." She let herself smile a little because the only part of this that was funny was the memory. "Are you talking about the Boynton brothers?"

Romeo snorted. "My very first bullies. Knowing what their life was like at home, I'm super-grateful that I got to grow up the way I did. And then you were there to pull them off me."

"That was only because they didn't think anyone would stand up to them. Especially a girl. And...come on, you were pretty scrawny in first grade."

"Oh, I remember."

"But you're not now." She took a chance and linked her arm through his. He stiffened a little before he drew his hand out of his pocket and slipped his fingers between hers.

"That's what I'm trying to say, Lil." His gaze settled on her face again and he frowned and chewed on the inside of his cheek. "The Boynton brothers didn't pick on me because of what I am. That part didn't matter. You were there to fight for me then, and I know you're trying to do the same thing now. But I..." He squeezed her hand and met her gaze squarely. "I don't need you to fight my battles for me. Especially this one, because it isn't a battle you can win. I'm a werewolf. The other magicals have their laws that apply to what I am, and there isn't a way to prove anything. There's no right and wrong because I can't change what I am or pretend to be something else."

Lily nodded and bit her lip. "But it is wrong to kick you out of an art museum simply for being what you are. You know that, right?"

"Of course I know that, Lily. Why do you think I try so hard not to pay attention to it?"

"You're right." She swallowed. "I'm sorry. I said I wasn't gonna bring this up again, and now we're talking about it—"

"No, it's okay. I only needed a minute to chill out first. Come here." He tilted his head and drew her toward him by the hand until they stood face to face. With his arms wrapped around her waist, she settled her hands against his chest and looked at him with a small smile. "I'll talk to you about anything. No secrets and no lies. I'm not trying to hide anything from you. I want you to know that."

"I do." Lily nodded and stared into his green eyes flecked with gold. "Same here."

"Good. That's...that's good to hear." Romeo smiled gently, and his whole face lit up. "Can we make a deal?"

"It depends on what it is."

He laughed. "I want to focus on going where we need to go. On finding your mom and figuring out who the hell doesn't want you to. Can we please...leave all this other stuff alone until then?"

"I think we can manage that." She raised an eyebrow in a teasing challenge. "On one condition, though."

"Oh, yeah? What's that?"

"If I find a way to make this a battle we can fight, will you fight it?"

He threw his head back for a short laugh. "Lily, if you can do that, you have free reign to handle it however you want. And I will be there with you through the whole thing." She raised her eyebrows and waited. "Yes. I'll fight it."

"Then you have yourself a deal, Mr. Stephens."

"Deal." He pulled her closer against him and kissed her—long and slow and gentle with relief and all his gratitude. She sighed and slid her hands up his chest to run her fingers through the dark curls at the nape of his neck. His arms tightened around her, and she pulled him closer until they seemed almost melded together.

I won't let this go—not Romeo and definitely not this stupid law about werewolves.

A small dog barked somewhere in the campsite. He grasped her hips, and she thought he intended to pick her up until the barking grew louder and closer.

"Charles, no!" a woman shrieked. "Charles, come."

Lily pulled away from the softness of Romeo's lips in time to see the tiny white dog barreling toward them across the concrete, the old woman hobbling after it. She laughed.

"Bad boy! Charles, no." The woman huffed along at a fairly impressive pace for someone in her eighties. The tiny white dog stopped in front of the couple and its entire body wiggled as it sniffed at Romeo's shoes and whined in excitement. The owner swatted a hand to her face. "I am so sorry. He's very friendly. And he's misbehaving. Charles, come." She clapped her wrinkled hands but the weak, muffled sound was swallowed by the noise of I-10 so close to the campground.

"It's totally fine," Romeo said, released Lily, and grinned at the woman. "Can I say hi?"

She stopped her apologies and stared at him with wide eyes. "Oh. Oh, of course."

He dropped into a crouch and offered the dog the back of his knuckles. "Hey, buddy." The little thing wiggled even harder, sniffed briefly, and attacked his hand with a volley of overexcited licks. "What's got you so riled up, huh?"

"He's excited to play," the woman said and shook her head. "We love this site. He knows every time we come through that he gets to see his friends."

"Oh, yeah?" He scratched behind the dog's tiny ears and ran a hand down the soft, curly hair.

"This KOA has a dog park." The woman nodded and raised an eyebrow at her pet. "One of the best we've seen, isn't it, Charles?" Her dog ignored her completely in favor of jumping up onto Romeo's knees and leaping unsuccessfully toward his face. "Get down!"

"It's okay." He laughed.

"I'm so sorry. He knows the rules. No jumping, Charles. I don't know *what's* gotten into him. Would you mind?" She held out her hands, both gnarled with arthritis.

"Sure." The tiny animal settled only when he scooped him into his arms and stood. Charles finally had the opportunity he wanted and lapped at Romeo's chin before he was deposited with care into his owner's arms. "Where's the dog park?"

"Over there." The woman cradled the dog to her chest and pointed. "He needs to run out some of this energy. And I need to stretch my legs. You two enjoy your evening. If this little scoundrel bothers you again...well, we're in the red Foretravel." She ruffled the hair on Charles' head and nodded at them.

"Have fun," he called after her but the woman was busy cooing admonishments to the tiny dog as she shuffled toward the fenced-in area at the end of the lot.

"Wow," Lily said.

"What?"

"That's the only red RV I see here." She pointed across the row in which they'd parked the Winnie.

He burst out laughing. "That's the most tricked-out rig I've ever seen."

"Maybe drop the RV lingo."

"Roll with it, Lil."

She grinned and shook her head. "What do they do with all that space? A tiny old lady and her tiny dog?"

"They're livin' in the lap of luxury." He took her hand again. "We'd better start saving for retirement now. I want one of those when I'm too old for stairs and too young for a nursing home."

"We?"

He grinned and planted another quick kiss on her lips. "Why not?"

"Okay...let's put the retirement conversation on the list of things to table until we find my mom, huh? Or even maybe, like...as long as possible."

"Oh, does it bother you to think about being old and retiring?"

"Maybe."

"Hey, don't worry. You'll be such a cute old lady."

She leaned away from him. "Oh, gross."

He pulled her back. "Way cuter than the one living in the red Foretravel." She laughed and pushed playfully against him. "And you won't even need a tiny, spastic dog to keep you company. You'll have me."

She threw her head back and laughed. "I can't even picture you as tiny and spastic."

"Yeah, but I'd be old too. You never know." Before she could escape, he licked her cheek.

"Oh, my God. Did you actually—"

Romeo caught her face with both hands and kissed her again, this time with far more urgency. She giggled until his tongue brushed against her lips and his heavy breath made her forget everything she wanted to say. When he pulled away a few seconds later, she was already breathless.

"I have two suggestions."

She laughed and rolled her eyes, her hand still around the back of his neck. "What?"

"I was going to say we should go check out the dog

park. I think it has the only green grass in El Paso, and I like dogs."

"Yeah..." Lily frowned and managed a hesitant smile.

"Or..." He turned his head and nodded over his shoulder at the Winnebago.

"Right now?"

"Yes, right now, Lily." He ran his thumb across her cheek and trailed it softly down the side of her neck before he brushed her hair back off her shoulder. His lips were hotter than the Texas air when he kissed her below her ear. He hesitated and whispered, "Unless you'd really rather go to the dog park." He couldn't get the whatever else he wanted to say out without chuckling.

She slapped his chest playfully and took his hand again. "Until you're tiny and spastic, that's never gonna be my first choice." With that, she dragged him after her toward the Winnebago's side door. She made it to the first step before he jerked her hand and spun her around again. The force of his kiss would've knocked her backward onto the second step, but he wrapped his arms around her again and climbed up after her. This time, they weren't interrupted before he lifted her off the living area floor. She wrapped her legs around his waist and kissed him fiercely while he carried her into the bedroom.

SIXTEEN

L ily woke the next morning to a growling stomach and the delayed realization that Romeo wasn't in bed beside her. With a long, languid stretch, she stared at the empty side of the bed and grinned. "I can't believe we never had dinner." Her stomach growled again. "Yeah, I know. I blame Romeo for that."

She threw the covers off and went to the doorway, where she'd dropped her purse the night before and never came back for it. "And that was...yep. Like sixteen hours ago." She retrieved her phone, opened the text from Romeo, and grinned.

Went out for breakfast. You can blame me for skipping dinner.

Shaking her head, she stepped out into the Winnie's kitchen and found the living space empty too. "I need a little something first..." The small Tupperware with three bran muffins was the first thing she saw in the pantry, so she went with one of those. After she'd placed it in the microwave for a few seconds and spread a little butter in the middle, she sat at the table with one of the best breakfasts in the world. "It doesn't even matter that I'm alone," she muttered with a shrug and picked a few crumbs off her plate before she took the last bite.

She had no sooner shoved the last piece into her mouth when the side door opened and Romeo stepped inside. "Wow, that smells amazing. What did you—oh. No. Get those things away from me."

Lily snorted and fought to keep from spraying muffin crumbs all over the small table. "It's gone," she said, holding a hand over her mouth. "I ate it all."

He raised an eyebrow at her and turned his head slowly to glare at the other two she'd left out on the counter. "You'll never win."

Laughing, she slid out of the booth and took her plate to the sink before she stored the muffins back in the pantry.

"But you..." He snaked an arm around her waist and pulled her toward him.

Her shout of surprise almost sent her mouthful of muffin all over him, but she covered her mouth and swallowed in one huge, painful gulp. "That's so dangerous," she said with a gasp.

"You're dangerous." He kissed her roughly, jerked back, and shook his head. "Trying to tempt me like that."

"Like what?"

"Mm...muffins."

She spun away from him and took a bottle of water from the fridge. "I wasn't betraying you. I promise. But I did give you all my attention last night, and my stomach was getting angry."

He raised an eyebrow and squinted at her. "A likely story."

Lily snorted. "What's in the bag?"

"Only El Paso's finest Mexican food open this early in the morning."

"Really?"

"Honestly, I have no idea. I might've even briefly stepped out of El Paso entirely."

She stepped toward the plastic bag on the counter to examine its contents. "It sounds like an incredible adventure."

"You have no idea." He moved behind her and settled his hands on her hips. "Full of danger." Leaning sideways, he looked at her. "And mystery." His lips hovered below her ear as he whispered, "And I did it all for you."

With a short laugh, she barely turned her head to raise an eyebrow at him. "If you're waiting for me to call you my hero..."

"Yeah, it was worth a shot." He gave her a quick peck on the cheek before he stepped aside to help her unload the to-go boxes. "I did bring you a feast, though."

"You know me too well."

THEY TOOK their time after breakfast to clean up a little, shower—which they were getting better at doing quickly, as they still hadn't fixed the four-and-a-half-minute cut-off time—and prepare to head out again. "You know, seeing as I don't know when we'll see actual grass after this, if you still wanna go to the dog park..."

Romeo looked at her from where he'd propped himself on the pillows in her bed, his hand behind his head and his feet crossed at the ankles. "Okay, there's gotta be something better to do around here. Something you wanna go see."

"I don't think so." She finished tying her hair back in a ponytail and glanced at him through the reflection in the wardrobe mirror. "I did see something about a water park, but my guess is it's overflowing with a horde of screaming kids on summer vacation and parents who'd rather be anywhere else." She eyed him a little longer until he took a sharp breath and shook his head.

"Yeah, you lost me at kids."

"Don't you like kids?"

"Kids are fine. When they're not being loud."

She laughed. "So you don't like kids unless they're sleeping."

"Sure." He grinned and scrambled from the bed. "Dogs, though, only get loud when they're trying not to be ignored. They don't go from zero to barking nearly as fast. Mostly."

"Does the same thing go for wolves?"

"Yeah, I'd say we have a higher threshold." Romeo wiggled his eyebrows. "Dogs like me and I like them."

"So, the dog park, then."

With a grin, he leaned forward in a half-bow and offered her his hand.

"We're gonna be the only people there without a dog," she said and slid her hand in his.

"No, we won't. Not at a concrete campsite right off the highway."

He was right. In the first two minutes, she counted three older couples seated on the benches under the park's awning, and none of them had leashes, doggie bags, or anything remotely pet-owner-like with them. There was only one family with a little five-year-old boy, who ran around with their Australian shepherd who made the boy fetch the ball half the time. Everyone else clearly watched their own pets running around on the soft grass.

A huge St. Bernard uttered a booming series of low barks at the next RV that drove past the park. "Dogs are loud," Lily said and nudged Romeo with her shoulder.

"You think that's loud, huh?" He tilted his head, his expression teasing. "Okay." Without explanation, he stood from the bench they'd chosen under the awning.

"What are you doing?"

Turning as he headed out onto the grass, he winked at her and grinned. Barely a few seconds later, the first two dogs that caught sight—or smell—of him darted away from whatever they were doing to investigate the stranger. He stretched his hand out to let them sniff him, gave them each a few pets, and laughed when the black lab tried to lean all its weight against his legs. Still laughing, he skipped sideways, and the dogs yipped and leapt after him.

In under a minute, he had almost every dog there chasing after him in playful bursts. All of them wagged their tails insanely and uttered the same excited whines he'd received from the tiny white dog named Charles. The dog owners were a little worried at first but eventually, they began to laugh at him too and enjoyed the sight of their pets having so much fun.

Lily sat on the bench and shook her head, but she couldn't keep from laughing with them. "National Geographic could make a whole new show outta this."

"Is he with you?" A middle-aged man wearing gray socks beneath his hiking sandals appeared beside her bench.

She tensed automatically but didn't want to repeat her mistake from yesterday with the man in the Stetson. This man, however, had a looped dog leash in his hand and looked away from her to immediately scan the park for his own pet. "Yep," she said, smiling at Romeo now bent halfway over and swung his arms out one after the other in playful attempts to swat whichever dog managed to get close.

"So which one's yours?"

"What?" The man nodded toward the yipping, barking pack Romeo had made for himself in the last five minutes. "Oh, no. We don't have any dogs, actually."

"Ah. I see. You're obviously dog people, though."

"Yeah, but now's not the right time. There's not enough time to focus on anyone else right now, you know? Even a dog."

"Even a dog." The man sidled closer to Lily's side of the bench and bent just a little toward her. "It looks like you have the next best thing."

"I'm sorry?"

"Being here. He gets to play with other people's dogs and leave 'em behind. I imagine it's rather like babysitting."

"And you're not a fan of babysitting, huh?" Lily chuckled.

"I've never done it before. Kids really aren't my style."

"This feels like déjà vu."

"Pardon?"

She shook her head. "Nothing."

"Well, when you're ready, you'll have everything you need. Remember that."

"Hey, you know, my mom used to—" Lily turned toward the man but he'd vanished. She scanned the little pavilion with the benches and the parking lot and swept her gaze over the dog park again, the gathered pet owners, and the one werewolf who soaked up all the canine attention on the grass. There weren't nearly enough people here for the man in socks and sandals to have vanished that quickly among them. "So another magical comes to give me sage advice without actually telling me anything." She snorted. "Romeo would've smelled that coming."

As soon as she said it, he straightened across the fenced-in patch of grass and met her gaze. He nodded, laughing, and waded toward her through the sea of yapping, bouncing, wagging dogs that demanded his attention.

I still don't know if that guy was talking about Romeo, dogs, kids, or...something else entirely. She raised her hand and wiggled her fingers at him. *It's not like it matters, anyway.*

THEY LEFT the El Paso KOA site a little after 1:00 p.m. after topping up the Winnie's gas tank and headed south to the border and Mexico and their final—for now—destination of Camargo. The traffic was much worse crossing the border there than it had been when they'd entered Canada.

"I'm so glad we don't have to forge my passport this time," Romeo muttered as they sat in the long line of cars and inched toward the crossing.

"We didn't forge your passport. I merely changed the expiration date."

"That's literally the same thing."

"You were really worried about that, were you?" Lily draped her wrist over the steering wheel and turned to grin at him.

"I'm amazed by the fact that you weren't, honestly."

"Didn't you tell me only a few days ago that it wasn't worth worrying about something you couldn't control?"

"You're absolutely right, Lil. Except it wasn't out of my control. I had total control all the way."

She laughed. "How's that?"

"I could've made the decision *not* to go across the US-Canadian border with a forged passport."

"Okay, okay. Well you don't have to worry any more at all about this, do you? Your shiny new passport is all ready to go and completely legal. There's nothing even remotely sketchy about it." She slapped her hand on their passports on top of the center console. "Including all the wrinkles and folds from how much you were beating up the old one before we crossed the first time."

"I'm allowed my own nervous habits, Lil."

"Yes. Yes, you are." She eyed him sideways and caught him smirking at her. "So this time, it should all be smooth sailing out of the country."

It was, for the most part—as long as they ignored the ridiculously long line and the much more thorough inspection of the Winnie before they were allowed to cross. Even with the AC on full blast, they still had to sit there with the windows rolled down and the side door left open for the border officer while he went through their belongings. By the time they'd answered every question and were cleared to drive through into Juarez, the back of her shirt was already damp with sweat and she had to wipe it off her forehead every thirty seconds.

"Thank God for AC," she said when the officer waved them through. She rolled both windows up and took her time to accelerate to the proper speed on the highway, which had now become Highway 45. "Hey, you did a much better job keepin' it cool this time."

"I wonder why." He rolled his eyes but mostly in jest. "I'm simply really glad they don't train their drug dogs to start barking at werewolves. Or the dozen other dog smells I have on me right now."

"You do kinda smell like a kennel."

His head whipped toward her. "Please tell me this is the first time you've ever thought that."

She laughed and shook her head. "It's definitely the first time. I gotta admit, I'm not exactly a fan of the eau de kennel, but I do like the way you smell. Normally. Not right now."

"Okay, I get it. I'll change when we stop next."

"That sounds good to me."

Romeo snorted, folded his arms, and leaned back into the passenger seat. "You like the way I smell, huh?"

"Oh, my God. Yes. Ninety-nine percent of the time."

His eyebrows twitched as he frowned. "What do I smell like?"

"Okay, I have no idea what werewolf smells like in general. Not like how you can pick up my magical-witch-Lily scent."

He chuckled and inclined his head. "I'd be a little worried if you did."

"Romeo, I've been around two werewolves in my entire life."

"Do you know what my dad smells like?"

She made a face. "That's not even—"

"Joking. I'm joking. That's also weird."

"Yeah, no kidding."

They were silent for a few minutes before he turned his head slowly toward her and leaned over the console. "So what do I smell like to you?"

"You know, whenever I put my finger on it, I'll make sure to tell you."

"Hmm." He studied her as if he thought he might press the matter, then straightened in his seat again. "Right."

She chuckled and eased her back to find a more comfortable driving position. *I dunno if I can come up with anything better. He smells like home.*

SEVENTEEN

I t took them a little over five hours to drive from the border to Camargo after almost an hour of sitting in the awful line of traffic simply to get into Mexico. At a quarter after seven, they passed a sign with the word *Camargo* on it. "And do you think that means we're there?" Romeo asked and laughed in disbelief.

"Well, that's the logical assumption."

"I thought you could speak, like...at least three other languages."

Lily glanced quickly at him before she returned her attention to the dry, sunbaked road stretching ahead of them. "I can. I'm fluent in French and Italian and...well, maybe semi-fluent in Russian. Spanish didn't quite make the list."

"You didn't learn Spanish?"

"Oh, I learned Spanish. You said you thought I could speak three other languages. I never really had an opportunity to practice Spanish."

"But you've been to Mexico."

"To a five-star resort, remember? Everyone there spoke perfect English. And it was a vacation."

"Wait, so lemme get this straight. You didn't have a chance to practice Spanish, but French, Italian, and Russian were ripe for the pickin'?"

She eyed him again, rolled her eyes, and smirked. "You have no idea."

"Well, please enlighten me."

"There's no secret. It was from all the galas and events my mom took me to, okay? Yeah, there were a few guest magicals from Spain, but Mexican Spanish is so different."

"Really?" He squinted at her and scrunched his face.

"Yeah. There's no lisp."

Romeo laughed. "What?"

"No lithp. In Spain—you know what? Never mind."

"Okay." He shook his head and looked at the navigation on his phone. "I guess we're evenly matched this time."

"What does that mean?" The only response from him was a shrug. "Okay, this isn't a competition or anything."

"Definitely not."

Lily looked away from the road for a few more seconds but couldn't tell if he was smiling sneakily or merely intently focused on the GPS. She flexed her fingers over the steering wheel. "So the drive down here was basically what I had expected."

"Yeah?"

"Dry. Empty. Virtually flat. Fair enough, we went

through those mountains if anyone can really call them that."

"Yeah, but look at that view." Romeo gestured dramatically toward the windshield and the wide, open expanse in front of them—scrubby bushes mostly brown and tan, an abundance of dirt, and the straight highway beneath the clear blue sky and a few puffy clouds that seemed to be utterly motionless.

"You and I have completely different definitions of a view."

"Hey, it all depends on how you wanna look at it."

Lily shrugged. "I guess I wouldn't mind it so much if it wasn't so stupidly hot."

"But you're sitting in a nice but outdated Winnebago that happens to have perfectly functional AC."

She sighed but had to laugh. "Okay. Point taken. The view's okay."

Shortly after that, the glistening buildings of Camargo came into view, along with more trees than they'd seen since Colorado. "It looks like we have some of that green you wanted," Romeo said. "There are two different rivers here. Didn't I say that when we headed out?"

"Yes." Lily fought back a smile. "Yes, you did."

Most of the city was made of low, squat adobe buildings with a few tall, white spires rising out of it. "Oh, my God. Those are palm trees," she muttered.

"Do you feel better about northern Mexico yet?"

"Eh...a little."

"Okay, you wanna take a right up here."

She followed his directions around the main part of the

city for another fifteen minutes. "Are you sure your GPS knows how to find this address?"

"Oh, yeah. I'm using a combination of the address and geographic coordinates. Plus good ol' map-reading in case."

"Boy, you're really on top of this."

"I know."

The buildings along the roads became a lot sparser, rising every quarter mile now from the brown, dry, desert valley. Finally, he leaned forward in his seat to squint through the windshield, double-checked his phone, and pointed. "That's it. On the right."

"Seriously?"

"Do you wanna see?"

"Nope. You're the navigator. I trust you. I merely didn't expect this." She pulled the Winnie up to a low wooden building with a slanted roof and a panel of tin as the front door. The whole structure was dusty and crooked and looked like it might collapse at any moment. There wasn't a name for the place or any other designated signs except for the rotting wooden planks nailed together over the door with squashed words in peeling black paint —*Beber. Comer. Hacer Nada.*

"I'm gonna take a wild guess and say this is a restaurant. Or a bar. Right off a Mexican freeway. Excellent."

"Why would that woman tell us to meet her at a bar, though?" Lily parked the Winnie next to the few other cars in the parking lot—which was, of course, all dirt. "I thought it was gonna be another house."

"You know, if random people called me from a different country, I'd have them meet me at a bar too."

"Yeah, okay. I simply thought she'd be a little more trusting of someone who deciphered that message in the basement with her phone number on it. How many people could've done that?"

Romeo unbuckled his seatbelt and grinned. "Well, I guess we'd better do this." He almost jumped out of the passenger seat to head out the side door, and Lily stuck the keys in her purse.

She paused and stared at her wallet sitting under her keys. "It's not hurting anybody, right?" After glancing briefly through the windshield and the driver-side window, she popped her wallet open and cast a small transformation spell on the twenty-dollar bill lying on top of her ID and the credit card Bentley had given her.

The knock on the driver's door made her jump. "Are you coming?" Romeo called and spread his arms wide.

Lily shut her wallet, slung her purse over her shoulder, and opened the door to slide out. "Romeo, we're at least forty-five minutes early. She said to meet her at eight, right?"

"Yeah. But if this place has food, I really don't wanna go another night without dinner." He winked, and she shut the door behind her. "Plus, I've never had a *Cerveza Mexicana* before. Or at least not a legit one."

"You're not gonna say it like that when you order it, are you?"

He smirked at her and took her hand. "Maybe."

"Please don't."

When they reached the front door, he chuckled.

"What?"

He pointed to another word painted in black on the tin door—*Abierta.* "I guess they're always open." She shook her head as he pulled on the makeshift handle that was basically little more than a large dry stick, and they stepped inside.

It was so dark in the small room that it took her eyes a second to adjust. The darkness didn't do anything to alleviate the heat and neither did the wide fan spinning with aggravating slowness in the center of the ceiling. The place smelled like sweat and dust mixed together, with a hint of alcohol. She swallowed. "I can't believe I'm saying this, but I think it's cooler outside."

"Well, at least we won't have a hard time finding a table." Out of all six of the tables in the long room that stretched farther back than seemed possible from the outside, only one of them was occupied. Two people sat at the bar in the back, and they both turned to look at the newcomers. One of them stood to walk behind the bar and waited there with a blank, dull expression.

Romeo gave her hand a little squeeze and all but tugged her across the one-roomed restaurant. *Maybe they serve food. I don't think it's a restaurant.*

"*Hola,*" he said when they reached the bar.

She glanced up at him with wide eyes. *He's gonna try to speak Spanish now, isn't he?*

The man behind the bar nodded and pressed his lips together.

"*Sirven la cena aquí?*"

The bartender's eyes narrowed and he glanced briefly at Lily before he shrugged casually. "*Empanadas.*"

"*Eso es?*"

His gaze flickered with some unrecognizable response before the man grabbed an overturned glass and a rag and started to wipe it with studied vigor. After a few moments of silence, he nodded.

"Okay." Romeo glanced at Lily and tilted his head. "*Empecemos con quatro.*" He held up four fingers. "*Y que hay de la cerveza?*"

She leaned back a little when the man's eyes grew incredibly wide and a huge grin spread across his face and altered it completely. "*Sí. Mucha cerveza.*"

Her friend chuckled. "*Solo dos, por favor.*"

"Okay." The man studied them for a few more minutes, raised his chin, and nodded at the dry wooden wall behind him. "*Quieren sentarte afuera? Hay mas aire.*"

"*Bueno.*" Romeo shrugged, smiled pertly at Lily, and nodded toward the bartender, who was now busy opening two beer bottles before he set them on the bar.

"*Venga.*"

Romeo picked up both beers, handed one to Lily and lifted his in a toast, and said, "We're gonna follow him."

She blinked, suddenly incredibly thirsty with the cold, perspiring bottle in her hand. "Did you—"

"Come on." He took her hand again, and they headed toward the bartender and the door he'd opened behind the building.

The evening light made Lily blink again and turn away for a minute, but she stepped outside behind Romeo and looked around slowly. "How did I not see this when we pulled up?"

"I think the building's a little wider," he said. "And you weren't looking for it."

"Were you?"

"No. But it's much cooler out here now."

They followed the bartender toward a low metal table in the corner of the restaurant's back patio, which was really another square of dirt haphazardly enclosed by a rough wooden fence. The six tables there felt a little too close together, but they all had to fit beneath the brown canvas tent erected above them on four rusty poles. The man pointed to the closest table and nodded.

"*Gracias*," Romeo said, pulled out a chair for Lily, and pushed it in again as she sat.

The man smiled again, nodded repeatedly, and seemed much happier now that they hadn't been turned away by their initial impression of his establishment. "*Uno momento.*" He turned away and disappeared inside the building again.

Romeo sat across from her and took a long sip of his beer. A huge sigh escaped him, and he lifted the bottle to give it an appreciative nod. "That tastes exactly like I thought it would."

"Okay, wait a minute." She leaned forward over the table and glanced around despite there being no one else on the back patio with them. "You said you didn't know any Spanish."

He leaned back in the metal chair and lowered his chin. "When did I say that?"

"Um...when I said I was fluent in the other languages."

Chuckling, he shook his head and took another sip of beer. "I said we were evenly matched."

"Yeah, with not being able to speak Spanish."

"Nope. I meant there's finally something I know that you don't."

"That's not evenly matched." She laughed.

"Okay. I lumped all your points for that together into one. To equal the one point I get for speaking Spanish."

She shook her head and stared at her beer. "I'll let you have this one. To being evenly matched, then."

"*Salud.*" They tapped their bottles together and drank. "Look at us. We made it to Mexico."

"Yes, we did." She took a deep breath and gazed out at the flat, sprawling landscape with nothing but horizon and sky. "Okay, maybe it's growing on me—wait. Where did you learn Spanish?"

"You might have gone to a fancy all-girls school, Lily, but I worked construction."

Her laughter faded completely as she closed her eyes. "I did not put two and two together."

"Most people in Charleston don't." With a final tip, he drained the rest of his beer, set it on the metal table, and eyed the back door into the restaurant. "I wonder how good the service is in a place like this."

"Do they have food here? Because I'm gonna need something with this *Cerveza Mexicana.*"

"Oh-ho. Listen to you."

"Shut up."

"Yeah, there's food. They have empanadas."

"Okay. And?"

Romeo met her gaze, snorted, and shook his head quickly. "No, that's it."

She simply laughed again and drank more beer. *If this is what Camargo's gonna be like while we're here, I'm fairly sure I'm okay with that. I hope that woman shows up, though.*

EIGHTEEN

By the time the bartender brought them one plate of four empanadas, three other tables on the patio had filled up. In the other corner of the squared-off outer area behind the restaurant, a man sat on a barstool and played a Mexican ballad. The woman seated beside him had a beautiful voice, and neither of them used an amp or microphones.

"She really has a great voice," Lily said. She bit into the hot, meat-filled pastry and sucked in a breath to cool it down. Another sip of beer helped with that. "I wish I understood the words."

Romeo shook his head and broke his first empanada in half. "I'd translate for you, but I don't really understand it."

"It sounds like Spanish to me."

"No, I mean..." He shrugged. "It's something about a cactus. And...I dunno. Maybe a toothpick?" She snorted. "Yeah. I don't get it."

"These are actually really good."

"Yeah, beer and empanadas for the win. We are getting down in Camargo."

She rolled her eyes, then froze. "Wait. What time is it?"

"Oh." Romeo pulled his phone from his back pocket before she could even get her purse from the back of the chair. "Seven fifty."

"Okay. We should probably be looking for the woman with no name and a phone number hidden in my mom's code language."

"Given how little we actually know about her, that's very specific." He grinned and bit into his food.

"Not specific enough." Lily studied the faces of everyone who'd arrived in the last twenty minutes, seemingly out of nowhere. "All these people have to be regulars, right?"

"Yeah. I don't think this place does very much marketing."

She coughed out a laugh and had to wash it down with more beer. "So whoever it is we're supposed to meet is bound to recognize us. It's logical that we kinda stand out." When she looked at him again, he'd stopped with his beer bottle pressed to his lips but only half tipped back. He raised an eyebrow. "Okay. I stand out."

"And I love it."

She inclined her head and smiled. "Well, thank you."

Neither one of them said anything else for the next five minutes. She was too focused on studying every new face that appeared on the back patio, looking for a woman who'd recognize them not as tourists but as the people who'd called her from Colorado. He was too focused on picking the crumbs off their plate and listening to the music.

Most of the restaurant's patrons hadn't even bothered to come through the front. They'd all stepped around the wooden building and climbed over the low wooden fence to reach the patio. Everyone seemed to know each other, too, which made sense, even for a bar so far removed from the main center of Camargo City. Lily glanced at her phone—7:59. "You know, she told us not to be late. I hate it when people don't follow their own—"

Her gaze settled on a woman in faded jeans, a white button-down shirt, and a dark-green trucker hat. She had one leg lifted over the wooden fence and her leather boot already planted in the dirt of the patio but she didn't complete the action to climb over it. Instead, she stared at Lily with wide eyes, her lips pressed together in a tight, grim line.

"Uh...Romeo?"

"I don't know, Lil. She'll show up."

"Yeah, I think I found her." She didn't look away from the woman, whose straight brown hair pulled back into a ponytail made her blue eyes stand out that much more. "Climbing the fence. Does she look terrified to you?"

He turned away from the musicians to scan the fence, then took a quick breath. "Yeah. A little."

As if his gaze had freed the woman from her frozen state, she glanced around the full patio, swung her other leg over the fence, and headed toward their table.

"That's gotta be her," he muttered.

"Yep."

The bartender passed in front of her, and she caught his arm and said something to him that Lily couldn't hear over the noise while she pointed toward their table. He nodded and in the next moment, the woman pushed the trucker hat on a little more firmly and pulled out one of the two open chairs. She sat between Lily and Romeo and looked at each of them in turn. "I hafta say I appreciate your punctuality."

Lily licked her lips. "Well, we did drive here from Colorado to be here at eight."

The newcomer glanced at their empty plate and the two empty beer bottles. "Quite a while earlier, it looks like." She stuck her hand out toward Lily. "Melissa Bore."

Finally. Lily took the woman's hand. "I'm—"

"Oh, I know who you are." Melissa's handshake was incredibly firm and a little brusque, and when she released her hand, she whipped the trucker hat off and smoothed her dark hair away from her forehead. "I wasn't completely sure over the phone, although I had an idea when you said Bentley sent you to me. But when I saw you..." The woman chuckled. "My God, Lily. You look so much like your mom. It scared me half to death."

She tensed. "You know my mom?"

"I did, yes. For a long time." The woman cast another furtive glance around the patio but no one seemed to pay them any attention. "I'm so sorry. I might be all the way down here, but any news about a woman like Greta Antony spreads everywhere." She punctuated the statement with a sharp chop of her hand and shook her head.

After a quickly shared glance with Romeo, Lily asked, "What news, exactly?"

Melissa sniffed, leaned back in her chair, and studied her for a moment. "She was...declared dead, wasn't she?"

"Yeah. Without any proof at all."

Folding her arms, the woman shook her head again. "That's awful. Again, Lily, I'm...so sorry. I wish I could've made it to the funeral."

"No, you don't." Lily sighed. "She would've hated it and told everyone to pull the sticks out of their asses already."

The other woman looked slightly taken aback for a moment, then barked out a laugh. "You're definitely her daughter." Romeo chuckled too, and she turned to him. "I'm sorry. Melissa."

"Oh. Romeo." They shook too, and he pretended to be more interested in getting the last drop of beer out of his second bottle. Lily saw his sideways glance at the woman and knew that he was watching her anyway, even if he didn't look directly at her.

Melissa laughed again, only more quietly this time and fiddled with the hat in her lap. "Greta was...one of the smartest, most stubborn witches I ever knew. She—" Another laugh escaped her. "She broke so many pieces of my furniture when we were working at this little apothecary outside of Greenville. I wanted to follow the recipes, right? If we were gonna sell potions to witches who couldn't get them anywhere else for miles, we had to do it right. But your mom..." She sniffed again, and her head twitched a little at the memory. "Greta told me to stop being an idiot and start thinking about how to make those recipes better. I tried, of course, but it was impossible to keep up with her. By the time I'd improved one or two, she'd had five new potions, from scratch, pulled out of her head to make something completely different that didn't even exist in the textbooks. Granted, she had about seven failures for every success. We had to move the lab to my basement simply to keep the mess contained. She actually burned my eyebrows off—twice."

Lily couldn't help but laugh at that. "That sounds like her. Only I never saw her mess up a spell or blow anything up with the wrong potion mixture."

The woman smirked. "Well, you only came into the picture after she'd already perfected everything she knew. Don't get me wrong. Your mom was always insanely talented, Lily. But she definitely had her rough patches. The learning curve applies to everyone."

Without an immediate reply, she simply nodded and studied her face. *She could be Mom's age. If I decide to believe what she's saying.*

"Oh. *Gracias*, Eduardo." Melissa nodded at the bartender as he set three more beers on their table.

He grinned at her. "*Cualquier cosa por ti.*"

"Ah." She waved a rough hand at the man and snatched her beer. "Get outta here." Laughing, he went off to tend to his other customers, and she lifted the beer to her lips for a few long, loud gulps. When she was finished, she took a huge breath and wiped her mouth with the back of a hand. "Those are for you, by the way." She wagged a finger at the other two bottles, which the couple both grabbed with thankful nods. "I'm glad you made it, Lily. If I have an opportunity to help Greta Antony's kid, I must be doin' something right down here."

She took a small sip of beer and frowned. "What are you doing down here?"

"Oh." Melissa nodded. "Yeah, I guess if Bentley sent you to the house on Iliff, he wouldn't know, either. And yes, I also know Bentley McClure. He went to school with my brother. We all ended up in different places, lemme tell ya. It doesn't make the world any bigger."

"When I called you the other day," Lily started, "I said I was looking for four-fifty-two."

"Right. And I can help you with that. I know I shouldn't be, seeing as you're your mom's daughter. But I'm actually impressed that you found my message and managed to decipher my number from the code."

"So you're the one who left it there."

"Yes, I am."

Lily nodded. "Was that your house?"

"You mean the charred carcass? Yep. My house and my place of business. My biggest goddamn mistake."

"What happened?" Romeo asked. Both Melissa and Lily turned to look at him, and he merely smiled.

"Yeah." Melissa sniffed and scratched the back of her head. "Everyone has their own answer to that question, don't they?" With a sympathetic smile, Lily offered a shrug. "Right. I ran a...kind of bank out of my home in Lakewood. For magicals, of course. And business was boomin'. It wasn't with actual money, though. More like a number of safe deposit boxes for all my clients. Your mom actually gave me the idea for the security system, Lily. Yep. I had the whole business running like a dream on three layers of protection wards—resistance barriers, invisibility, the works. A few of my clients wanted DNA-tailored locks. No problem. And I rigged up this really cool process —a totally specific mix of summoning and exclusion at the same time. I came about as close as I ever got to teleportation through potions, honestly. It took a while to get through all the different layers, so I had about a twenty-four-hour mandatory notice if anyone wanted any of their—"

She stopped, her hands that were so animated while she spoke now frozen in front of her. "I am not answering your question, am I? And you don't really care about the specifics." She clapped her hands together and nodded. "Safe deposit boxes. I handled this for virtually every magical who needed a safe, hidden place for their valuables in...oh, ten states, at least. Then, it all went to hell." She shook her head and took another long sip of beer. "Let's say I provided services to the wrong vampire. I didn't know what I was getting into until it was too late. He tried to strongarm me. And then he tried to break into my vault, so I had to split."

"Did this vampire try to break in first and then set your house on fire," Lily asked.

"I'd put money on it."

"I'm sorry. That sounds awful." She took another sip because she didn't want to look like a crazy person who enjoyed other people's misfortune. *I knew it.*

"But you went back after the fire to leave that message," Romeo added.

"What?" Melissa shook her head. "No. I knew that undead thug was coming a day before he showed up. I left the message then, and by the time he thought he knew how to break through my wards, I was already gone."

"Then someone else went through your house after the fire and took a few things," Lily said. "There were pictures missing from the wall in the dining room."

"Meh." Melissa shrugged. "Whoever it is can keep whatever they took. There was nothing in that house I needed anyway once I left."

"Except for all your clients' valuables, right?" Romeo cleared his throat when the woman studied him for a few seconds longer than seemed appropriate.

She chuckled and nodded sarcastically at him. "You're funny. Of course I didn't leave all their stuff behind. Most of it was incredibly volatile and would do serious damage to thousands of people if—" She forced out a cough and drank. "No, I set the whole thing up to come down here with me. Every item and every client collection. They all knew the protocol to find me if anything should happen. Which it did. That was all part of my contract. But you two had absolutely no idea what you were looking for and you still found it." She pursed her lips and hunched over the table. "Which makes me think I should've made it harder to find."

"No, believe me. It wasn't easy," Lily said. "We were down there for, what? A couple of hours?" She glanced at Romeo and he nodded.

"Something like that."

"Half of it was spent trying to find your message. The other half was me tying my brain in knots trying to find some kinda pattern in the numbers you left after I deciphered them."

Melissa grinned. "So how did you discover it was a phone number?"

"Telemarketers," Romeo said. Lily snorted.

The other woman looked curiously at him and nodded. "Well, you get points for giving me an answer I've never heard before."

He smirked and glanced at Lily. "She works on a point system too. I like this witch."

"Ha. I seem to be building a following down here."

"What?"

"It doesn't matter. It's good to know you guys had to work extra hard to get in touch with me. I only hope that jerk without a heartbeat isn't nearly as smart as he thinks he is. Or as either of you are, apparently."

"That would be difficult," Romeo said with a chuckle.

Melissa flicked her gaze toward him, and her smile vanished. "Have you ever messed with a vampire?"

He frowned. "No."

"Good. Don't underestimate those creeps. That's why I hightailed it to Mexico. I heard somewhere that they don't like being this close to the equator. There's way too much sun."

Lily pressed her lips together and clenched her jaw. *If I laugh, I don't think she'll feel bad about calling this meeting off.* "So you brought all your clients' valuables with you," she said instead in an effort to lead the conversation back on track.

"I sure did. Oh. And that's why you're here." Melissa slumped an elbow onto the table and leaned forward toward Lily. "four-fifty-two."

"four-fifty-two." Lily nodded.

"Your mom had a box in my vault, Lily. I'd already been rockin' the business for a while before she arrived three, maybe four years ago. But the fact that Greta trusted me enough to keep her things safe fully convinced me I was doin' something right." Lily held her breath and Melissa's gaze. "Four-fifty-two is hers."

NINETEEN

The patrons on the patio behind the nameless restaurant talked and laughed, apparently without a care in the world. The musicians continued to play, perhaps even louder now they had a bigger audience. Lily only heard those few words. *Four-fifty-two was hers.*

Both Romeo and Melissa stared at her and waited for her to say something—to give any kind of reaction at all. She swallowed. "You still have it, right?"

"Do I still—" The woman shook her head like a fly had landed there and regarded her with an expression that seemed to be a mixture of offense and disbelief. "I would not have pushed you down memory lane if I didn't have something to show for it at the end. Or told you to come all the way down here. Of course I still have it, Lily."

"I had to ask." They stared at each other for a few seconds before the older woman burst into piggish snorts of laughter.

"I know you did. Let's get started, then, huh? We have

a lotta work to do before you decide whether or not this trip of yours was worth it." She threw back the rest of her beer, belched, and shrugged as she stood from the table. "Come on."

The young couple exchanged another glance, and he nodded to where the woman made her way across the patio again. Lily retrieved her wallet from her purse, opened it, and took out the Mexican bills with her own magical exchange rate of zero. The two-hundred-peso bill seemed like enough, so she set it on the table under her empty beer bottle and stood with Romeo.

"When did you get pesos?" he asked.

"Uh...right before I got out of the Winnie."

He frowned at her and did a double-take before he glanced at their empty table. "You magicked your money?"

"So we could pay for our food. And the beer."

He stared after her for a minute, his expression blank. Then, he nodded. "Okay, that's a good reason to do it."

She grinned at him. "I know."

"Oh, hey." Melissa whirled to face them. "I forgot to mention I have a tab with Eduardo. So any time you wanna stop by again before you leave this fantastically desolate little place outside the city, let him know it's on me." She winked. "I covered your empanadas too."

Lily sighed but couldn't help a wry chuckle. "I guess I've left a really big tip."

"I don't think anyone's gonna condemn you for that, Lil."

A loud, metallic bang distracted them. Melissa's hand rested against the cab of a seriously beat-up gray pickup that tilted slightly to the right. "You'll wanna follow me closely, all right? Just so everyone knows I actually want you to follow."

"Got it," Lily called as they turned toward the Winnie. "How many people follow her in the first place?"

"I can't even pretend to have an answer for that. Do you want me to drive?"

"Yep." She handed the keys over, and they scrambled into their seats again and followed the gray truck to one more thing Lily's mom wanted her to find.

Their guide turned right onto the road, away from Camargo City. They drove for another ten minutes and saw absolutely nothing around them but scrubby bushes and a few low, squat buildings in the distance. The only other turn they took was left onto an unmarked road. Lily frowned at the almost-desert. "Okay, so I get it that an unnamed road is the whole point. She's trying to hide from...vampires, I guess. Still..."

"I know." Romeo glanced at his side mirror. "It kinda creeps me out too. At least no one's following us."

After another ten minutes, they reached a collection of short, square adobe buildings. The older ones with more cracks and a few holes were arranged in a semi-circle around the end of the unnamed road. Newer buildings— darker with less time baking under the intense sun—had been added around the perimeter, but there were enough structures to make it appear disorganized. Chickens pecked at the dirt and a few blades of dead brown plants and strutted carelessly away from the main road when

Melissa's truck rolled slowly past and kicked up a constant stream of fine dust.

"Do you know what this place makes me think of?" Romeo asked and studied the empty, stacked wooden crates beside one of the buildings.

"What?"

He glanced at her and smirked. "*The Three Amigos.*"

She snorted. "That shouldn't be funny."

When they reached the end of the main road, the woman ahead took another left turn and drove across the scrubby brush and packed dirt. "Off-roading." Lily caught a glimpse of a young woman's face peeking out from behind a brightly colored blanket hung over an open door-way. "And people watching us."

"My advice would be to not watch them back." Romeo cleared his throat. "Until we know exactly where we are." He sniffed, frowned, and smelled the air again.

"Melissa's obviously a witch." She watched the confusion grow on his face. "Do you smell someone else's magic?"

"Not even a little." His nostrils flared, and his grip tightened on the steering wheel.

"So what is it?"

He simply stared directly ahead and followed the gray truck as it rolled slowly between the low buildings. "Were-wolves. A large pack, too. And...something else I have never picked up before."

"Oh. Well, it's good that you recognize one of them, at least."

"Not really." He glanced quickly at her before he squinted through the windshield again. "I've never been part of a pack, Lily. That's what we're driving into right now. And they—" He sniffed again, started to turn his head to look out the window, but thought better of it. "They know what I am too."

Lily took a deep breath. "Is this gonna be more trouble than it's worth?"

"What? Definitely not. We're doing this. It simply... might be more trouble than we want."

"Okay..."

He looked at her again and offered a tight smile he meant to be reassuring. "Don't worry. We only hafta keep our heads down more than usual. Do what we came here to do and get out."

"I'm not worried." She studied the frown that seemed to have almost become a permanent feature. "I haven't ever seen you so on edge."

"This is me being cautious. You'll know on edge when you see it."

Finally, Melissa stopped her vehicle in front of a single-story adobe house that resembled all the others in what seemed to be a small settlement. The truck's brakes squealed and it rocked dangerously when she stepped out onto the dirt and waved them toward her. They exchanged a glance and he turned the Winnie off and handed her the keys before they got out.

The desert valley around them was washed in the orange-pink glow of sunset, the dirt and sand studded now with the black dots of coarse brush. It made all the buildings look pink in the light and brown-red where their shadows fell. The air was so dry, her nose felt raw.

The older woman stood in front of the solid wooden door of this particular house, surrounded by rows of potted cacti and some other desert plant Lily didn't recognize. "I've had a few of my clients contact me since I made the move," she said, the trucker hat back on her head now and her arms folded in a no-nonsense gesture. "I haven't brought any of them to my home, though." She nodded at her. "I'm happy to make exceptions for Greta's daughter. But you two need to know that all bets are off if you tell anyone where I am."

"Well, no one knows we're here, anyway," she replied. *Maybe I should've called Bentley and told him about the slight change of plans.*

Licking her lips, Melissa nodded. "Good. I can be more help to you that way. Step a little closer, please." They both did as they were told, and the woman reached out with a glowing blue light at the tip of her fingers to touch each of them on the shoulder. "You don't wanna set off any alarms, right?" She smirked, turned, and pushed the door.

Romeo cast a quick glance over his shoulder to check that no one had approached, although he felt eyes everywhere. Lily stepped through the door first, and he followed. The minute it closed on its own behind them, he stumbled a little, righted himself, and was attacked by a fit of sneezing.

"Oh, that was stupid of me." Their host flashed him an apologetic look and plucked a purple flower from the planter hanging from the ceiling. She handed it to him. "If you eat that, it'll help the symptoms."

He didn't hesitate and simply crammed the flower into his mouth, chewed quickly, and swallowed. "It tastes like cinnamon," he said and sounded surprised.

"Only to you, kid."

He sent Lily an exasperated look. *Yeah. She actually called him kid.*

"What was that?" she asked.

Melissa raised her hand to check a few of the other potted plants overhead, their vines and fronds and flowers dangling over the sides. Honestly, the woman's house looked more like a garden warehouse than a potions shop or a magical bank. "That was wolfsbane."

"Uh...isn't that poisonous?" She glanced quickly at her friend.

"Incredibly," the woman replied and continued to pay more attention to her plants than her guests. He coughed. "But not for werewolves. That flower is the only thing I know that combats the effect strong magic has on your race, Romeo. It's funny. I've heard recovering alcoholics talk about having an allergy to booze. I assume magic is something of the same for your wolf." She finally looked at him and nodded. "Do you feel it?"

Romeo swallowed, and once he'd gotten over the surprise of thinking he'd been poisoned, he paused. "Yeah, actually. It's much better." He took a deep breath and didn't feel like he'd downed half a pint of whiskey. "Did you discover this"—he sniffed again—"cure?"

"Oh, it's definitely not a cure. It'll wear off in about five hours. So it's up to you whether or not you wanna keep treating that allergy of yours. I have plenty so let me know if you want more."

Lily's attention was drawn to the long, low bench built into the right wall. It was completely filled with different-colored vials, stoppered bottles, beakers and jars, glass tubes, plastic sample cups, metal bowls, and a huge tub at the very end housing more of the same, all of which were clearly sealed and labeled in a tiny script she couldn't read from where she stood. She opened her mouth to ask about the potions lab, but she didn't get the chance.

"Wait a minute," Romeo said and shook his head as the fog of his reaction to magic lifted even more. "I didn't smell any of this magic outside and I'm usually good at finding it."

"I'm sure you are." Melissa turned toward him and stuck a hand on her hip. "But I'm exceptionally good at hiding it. I'd have to be an incredibly stupid witch to come all the way down to Mexico with my vault of magical items and not put a lid on it. This place would essentially be a homing beacon for any magical who might want to take what doesn't belong to them. Like that goddamn vampire. Not to mention how dangerous it would be for me personally, what with all the werewolves in the neighborhood." She chuckled. "I put three different series of containment spells around this house. And a variation of—sorry. I get carried away with the process."

He frowned, rubbed his forehead, and lowered his hand with a thump against his thigh. "Yeah, that's what I was getting at. So why are you out here with your containment spell but, living with a werewolf pack?"

"It's a little unexpected, huh?"

"Uh, yeah."

"Good." Melissa nodded and pointed at him. "I'm glad it threw you off. I didn't come down here as a tourist, remember? And what better way to blend in than to make a new home for myself with a small, reclusive community of locals who don't really get out much?"

He glanced at Lily, who merely shrugged, and he squinted at the potions witch. "That doesn't really answer the question."

"Sure it does. But okay, I'll spell it out for you. No one's gonna go looking for a witch with serious firepower under her belt, so to speak, smack-dab in the middle of a wolf den in Nowhere, Chihuahua. I hide in plain sight surrounded by the enemy."

Lily's head whipped toward her. "Enemy?"

"Whoops. Nope. Sorry. I only meant it as far as magical law and the stuck-up, privileged lawmakers are concerned. You know, exclusionary provisions against werewolves as an entire race is one of the dumbest things I've seen in our world. It's like throwing a huge party with tons of booze and making it a strict rule—no drunks allowed. Not all drunks are bad people. Not all drunk people are drunk all the time. And not all bad people are drunks. Right?"

Lily took a deep breath, paused, and puffed out a sigh. "I'm gonna take your word on that one."

"Well, you can. Listen, I know there's nothing wrong

with werewolves, only with the system. Your mom knew that too, Lily. She also knew many werewolves in her day who she didn't try to turn away, no questions asked, simply because of some idiotic decree. Granted, when a wolf acts like a crazy person around tons of concentrated magic in one place, things can get a little out of hand. But that's merely biology, not a crime. And none of those uppity-ups wanna take the time to find a way to make it better for everyone, only themselves." The woman paused and shook her head vigorously before she blew out a huge breath. "And I'm getting way off topic." She pointed at Romeo again. "I'm here because it feels like the last place anyone I don't want to find me is gonna come lookin'."

He stared at her. "And they simply let you move right in."

Melissa chuckled and rolled her eyes. "Well, not without a little compensation. Come on. I'm no freeloader. We worked out a deal, and I'd say it benefits everyone quite nicely."

"What kind of deal?" Lily swept her gaze over the house, which she only now realized had to be magically enhanced on the inside because it was much bigger than it should have been.

The woman cleared her throat. "This particular pack requires a certain type of containment ward. In their line of business, they tend to need these. Frequently. And I grow them wolfsbane." She pointed to the planter. "Other than that, I don't ask about their business and they don't ask about mine."

What kind of containment wards would a pack of were-

wolves need? When Lily glanced at Romeo, she knew he wondered the same thing.

"Great." Their host sniffed, tugged her trucker hat off, and tossed it on a small desk in the center of the room that doubled as supply counter, kitchen table, and all-around junk surface. "So now we all know what Melissa Bore's doing in Mexico and why. Lily, I'd say it's time to pull out your mom's deposit, don't you think."

She nodded and took a deep breath. "Definitely."

TWENTY

"All right. You two find some chairs and sit, huh? You're making me nervous." Melissa laced her fingers and pushed her knuckles back, cracking all of them at the same time.

Lily glanced around. *Either I'm going crazy, or she already has.* "Uh, where are the chairs?"

"They're over—oh. Yeah, I put those away." The potions witch—who obviously had an affinity for security wards and hidden charms—clapped her hands and gestured like she took hold of two door handles at the same time and jerked them open. The air on the other side of the single room shimmered and two simple wooden chairs winked into existence in what very little open space existed in the house.

The couple crossed the room quietly to take their seats as instructed. Melissa clapped again and loud salsa music began to play. Lily couldn't find where it was coming from. "Wanna bet she has a magical sound system too?" she muttered and leaned toward Romeo in the chair beside her.

"I don't wanna bet anything." His wide eyes remained on Melissa for a minute before he turned toward his companion. "I don't understand half of what she says. And the other half is plain weird."

"I know." She watched the woman, who now danced a cha-cha across her house and gathered various items from the hanging planters, the tall shelf against the back wall, and the bench full of vials and beakers. She didn't seem to have a designated workspace—or she'd turned her entire house into one—and simply dumped whatever she was looking for into the same metal bowl cradled in the crook of her arm. A little hum escaped her lips, but it didn't match the salsa music at all. "But I believe her. She said she knows my mom. I guess she still doesn't know that it's actually present tense."

"Are you gonna tell her?" Romeo folded his arms and squinted as he watched the woman dance and work and embody as much oddity in her actions as she did in her speech.

"Maybe. If she's really not jerking us around or something doesn't go horribly wrong. The stories about blowing up furniture didn't exactly make a great case for her."

He chuckled. "Those stories were about your mom."

"Yeah. And they were friends. Look at this place. I can't even make sense of her labeling system if that's even what it is. There's no organization to anything. I bet she's blown up a few things in her time too."

"Hey, if you were hiding from a vampire who wanted

to destroy your livelihood—and possibly you too—do you think you'd be able to keep everything nice and neat?"

She stared at him as if she thought the question irrelevant. "I don't know. But I am trying to track my missing mom, who everyone else really thinks is dead, while trying not to be killed by any more witches calling me a loose end. And the Winnie's very clean."

He snorted and shook his head. "You're merely able to juggle many different things, Lil. You're good with that stuff. Just because a person's messy, though, doesn't mean they're not also good at what they do."

"Oh, I know." She tilted her head at the sight of Melissa standing with one foot on a precariously rickety table and the other propped against a stack of books while she reached for something on the top of the shelf on the back wall. "But I don't understand it."

"At least you can recognize it." He smacked his lips and his tongue flicked out a few times.

"Are you okay?"

"Yeah, it's the...uh, cinnamon. Don't get me wrong. I don't have a problem with it but it's weird when that's the only thing I can taste."

"Do you still feel okay?"

"Oh, yeah." He grinned. "I'd be down with tasting cinnamon for the rest of my life if it means I don't get so ridiculously messed-up around magic. I can still smell it, though, and kinda feel it in the air." Again, he took a few quick sniffs. "But my head's totally clear." Laughing in surprise, he leaned forward and propped his elbows on his thighs. "Wolfsbane. How does every werewolf on the planet not know what this stuff does?"

"Well, either Melissa's the only witch who's discovered it, or someone's put a few things in place to keep werewolves from finding out about it."

Romeo turned his head to look at her. "Like the Council."

"Like the Council." Lily shook her head. "They should be trying to help you, Romeo, not sweep you all under the rug."

"Lily—"

"Yeah, I know. I promised to let this go until after we find my mom. So I'm simply gonna say this. I think Melissa Bore might have found a way to make it a fight we can win."

His mouth dropped open with his next breath, and his eyes scrunched—like it hurt him to think that far ahead into the future. "Okay. We can come back to that idea later."

"Okay."

<hr>

THE NEXT TIME Lily thought to pull out her phone for the time, it was a little after 10:00 p.m. As far as she could see, Melissa's house didn't have any windows—at least from the inside. As a result, she'd completely missed the transformation of sunset into complete darkness but it had to be dark outside. *The no-windows thing really makes it easy to lose track of time in here.* She and Romeo sat through the woman's salsa-music phase, followed by techno-jazz, and the last two tracks playing through Melissa's magical sound system were some version of heavy metal and symphony woven together. *No wonder she's so eccentric...in a weirdly understated way.*

Finally, the potions witch seemed satisfied with what she'd whipped together in her metal bowl, which had gone through multiple rounds of flashing in different colors, bubbling over onto the desk-table without leaving the expected mess behind, and even mixing itself once or twice. "Ah. Do you smell that?" It was the first thing she'd said and the first time she'd looked at either of them since she officially began the process neither of them understood.

"Uh... it smells like popcorn," Lily said flatly.

Romeo looked at her and tilted his head. "Huh. I'm getting burnt rubber."

"Really? Interesting." Melissa grinned and raised an eyebrow. "You know, after all this time, it still amazes me how specific the outcome is to each person. I love it." She swirled the contents of the bowl a few more times and took a long, deep whiff of it. "For me, this one's poppin' anise, peppermint, cumin, a hint of fish oil, and...yeah. Dirty socks."

Lily frowned. "That's not a drinking potion, right?"

The woman threw her head back and barked out a sharp laugh. "You are Greta all over again, girl. A few inches shorter, maybe, but as plucky." Her laughter died instantly, replaced by a sharp, piercing gaze aimed at the younger woman. "No. This is not a drinking potion. Not unless you wanna send your spleen to an alternate dimension. I think." She set the bowl down on the table, cleared everything else away, and dumped the excess random mess on any other surface close at hand. "Well, come on, then. Get over here." She beckoned them to join her and nodded encouragement.

Lily groaned when she pushed out of the stiff wooden chair. "I can't believe I sat in this the whole time and did absolutely nothing." Romeo chuckled and stood beside her. She thought she caught him wince despite his apparent humor at her expense.

They approached the witch at the table and stepped close to peer cautiously into the metal bowl. "That looks like blood," he muttered.

"Isn't it beautiful? Okay, Lily. Your mom was one of my clients who used my DNA-tailored lock system for accessing her things. Normally, I'd only need a strand or two of hair, you being her daughter and everything."

She looked at the woman and bit her lip.

"So...a strand or two of hair? Do you want me to pull it out for you?"

"Oh. You said normally. I thought this was something different."

Melissa chuckled. "It's definitely different. But we can't go different without starting at the basics. Let's have it." Lily fingered a few strands at her hairline. It was harder than she expected to take hold of only a few and not a whole chunk but she finally managed three and offered them to the other witch. "Dump 'em in."

She dropped her hair into the red sludge that did actually look like blood, and the strands were quickly sucked under the surface. The potion in the bowl rose with a single large bubble in the center. When this popped, it uttered a startlingly human-sounding cough. She blinked and glanced at Romeo, who shrugged and shook his head.

"Excellent." Their host nodded and smoothed her dark hair away from her forehead. "Now we move on to the not-so-normal. Greta asked me if I could add an extra-extra layer of security to her box. I didn't quite understand it at the time, and I still don't, honestly. I mean"—she chuckled—"how could you be you and not you at the same time? Whatever. But the extra security needs an extra key, so to speak." She leaned forward over the table and squinted at Lily. "Do you got anything of your mom's that might work?"

"Um...it depends on what kinda thing, I guess."

"Oh, something she's been in contact with—touched or used or had some kinda magical effect on. Works even better if it means something to both of you."

She frowned. "Okay, all I really have of hers is a collection of old pictures from when I was—oh. Wait." She fumbled in her purse still hung over her shoulder and dug around until she heard her keys jingle. With her next attempt, she located the keychain and pulled it out. There was the keyring charm—now one solid piece of metal again in the shape of a maple leaf with *Mont Tremblant National Park* stamped across it in capital letters. "This'll probably work." It took her a few seconds to work the charm off the keyring, but she finally handed it over to the witch and folded her arms.

The corners of Melissa's mouth pulled down as she studied the little trinket and turned it over. "Mont Tremblant?"

"It's in Canada," she explained.

"Huh. Did you and Greta take a special trip out there or somethin'?"

Lily glanced at Romeo. He smirked and looked at the potion bowl. "Kinda."

The woman clicked her tongue. "You Antony women. I don't get it. You kinda took a trip together and kinda didn't." She blew a raspberry and shook her head. "This'll probably work."

"Is it—I mean, will I get that back afterward?"

"Why? Is it important to you?"

She startled. "You only said you needed—"

"Ha! I'm joking. You'll get it back when all the locks are open and the magic has worked itself out. Probably." Melissa shrugged and plopped the charm into the metal bowl. It sank quickly to the bottom with a metallic clink, but nothing else happened.

"Did it work?" Lily stared at the thick red sludge.

"I have no idea." The older woman sniffed. "We won't know until the morning. These things have a twelve-hour delivery time." She snorted and looked at the couple like they should've caught the obvious joke. "Okay, then. It's..." She glanced at her battered watch. "Ten seventeen. This time tomorrow morning, you should have box four-fifty-two."

"We should or we will?"

"Yeah, I can appreciate your skepticism. You'll have it

in the morning, Lily. If nothing else, I owe it to your mom to get you what you need. I simply like to have a little fun, right? But under all that, I know what I'm doing. You can trust me."

She studied the woman's bright blue eyes for a few seconds longer but finally nodded. "Okay."

"Okay." Melissa glanced from one to the other as if waiting for them to say something. "Oh. Well, I'd offer you a place to stay for the night, but all my spare rooms are full at the moment. Not with other guests. Merely...valuable things." She glanced at the ceiling as if to listen for something they couldn't hear. "Hey, but you brought your beds with you, huh? Or...bed. Ah, that's none of my business. Do you need to hook up to anything? I have no problem if you two park that giant boat on wheels outside my door overnight."

"No." Lily shrugged and glanced once again at the red sludge in the bowl. "We haven't had to use the generator in a while, so I think we're good for a night." She turned to Romeo for confirmation, but he frowned at the potions witch.

"What about your neighbors?" he asked.

"Hmm. What about them?"

"Will they have a problem with us camping out? They didn't seem very happy to see us drive through."

"Oh, they don't seem very happy about anything, not even when they come to me. You're all right, though. As long as you're outside my door, they know you're here for business or at least as a guest. They won't bite you for it." She chuckled at her own awful wordplay.

"So." Lily spread her arms and smiled. "I'm exhausted. Sleep sounds remarkably good right now while we wait."

"Sleep makes everything better in the morning," the woman said. "If you can get it. Would you like me to walk you out?"

"No." She tried not to laugh and glanced at the only other door in the single room. "I think we got it."

"Great. See you in the morning. If you need anything, knock. Actually, I might not hear you so come on in and shout for me. That usually works."

"Okay." She nodded at Romeo, and when they turned away from the table to head toward the door, her eyes widened. *This woman's all over the place.*

His hand slipped into hers and he called over his shoulder, "Have a nice night."

"Oh, you too." The heavy-metal-symphony mix began to play again when they reached the door but it cut off abruptly once they stepped outside and she shut it behind them.

She stared at the adobe walls and the wooden door. "I think she's sound-proofed the whole thing too. Exactly like the speakeasy in Canada."

"At least she realizes playing all her super-loud music might not earn her any points with the neighbors." He paused on their way to the Winnie and sniffed the air again.

"Are you okay?" She didn't see anyone, but the fact that there weren't any streetlights out there—or any lights on at all—made it difficult to see anything.

"Yeah. Let's get inside." He squeezed her hand and

didn't relax until they were in the RV with the side door shut and locked from the inside. With a huge sigh, he slumped onto the couch and ran a hand through his curls. "This is so weird."

"So, I have the feeling you're not actually okay." Lily sat beside him on the couch and pulled her legs up to cross them on the cushion. "What's going on?"

Romeo tilted his head side to side. "Beyond all the weird potion-making we watched and the fact that there's a poisonous antidote to my magic allergy?" she snorted and clapped her hands over her mouth. He smirked. "Okay. I like that last part. The really weird thing is being here with so many other werewolves. Honestly, I'm reasonably sure that includes everyone here except you and Melissa. I can feel them...well, it's not really like watching me. Sensing me, maybe? Trying to figure me out or read me or..." He sighed. "I don't know what it is. But I have a sense that there's something else going on here in this little compound or whatever that isn't quite right."

"Like what?"

"I dunno, Lil. It's only...it makes me feel itchy." His entire body tensed and he shuddered.

"Well, once we get my mom's magical safe deposit box in the morning, we can hightail it outta here, okay? I don't think I really wanna stick around much more than that, either."

"Not even to hang out with one of your mom's old friends?"

"What? Well, it's nice to hear stories about her from way back when but—oh. You were totally kidding."

He snorted. "Yeah."

"Right. You know, it's kinda hard to imagine my mom and Melissa hanging out together, whipping up spells, and being friends. My mom has her quirks, of course, but she's fairly normal. Melissa's...I dunno. Maybe that's what happens when you spend all your time keeping everyone else's secrets and having to run away because of them."

"Maybe she sniffed a few too many potion fumes."

A laugh burst out of her, and she shoved his shoulder. "That's awful. And totally possible, I think."

He laughed too, caught her hand, and pulled her into his lap. "Did you ever mess around with potions like that?"

"Are you trying to ask me if I've done the magical equivalent of sniffing glue?" He shrugged and wrapped his arms around her. "The answer is no. I can make a potion if I have to, but honestly, the really powerful ones take longer to accomplish. I'm simply not that patient."

"Hmm. Me neither." His hand slid behind her head and he pulled her down toward him for a long kiss. When he pulled away again, he frowned at her looked a little nonplussed. "You taste like cinnamon."

She shook her head. "That's not me."

"Huh. Maybe there's one downside to wolfsbane, then."

"Can you handle it?"

"Oh, yeah." He lifted her in his arms as he stood from the couch and headed toward the bedroom. "The question is, can you?" She merely kissed him in response and let him carry her to bed.

TWENTY-ONE

Lily woke before sunrise with a sense of expectation. The blue glow of the fading night peeked through the curtain in her bedroom window. She rolled over to drape her arm over Romeo's hips but it thumped onto the bedsheets in the empty space beside her instead. Her mind registered what that meant and she forced herself to open her eyes and stared at the rumpled sheets where he was supposed to be. *There's no way he took a walk to get breakfast this time.*

"Romeo?" She sat and listened. The silence above the hum of the generator was pierced by rising howls from somewhere out in the desert.

That is definitely a pack of wolves.

"Romeo?" When he still didn't answer, she tossed the covers aside and rose from the bed. The Winnie was still mostly dark without any sunlight, so she flipped the lights on in the living area and blinked against the glare. "Are you in here?" She once again received no response.

The eerie call of many howls in unison came again.

In her pajama shorts and tank top, she opened the Winnie's side door—which was unlocked now—stepped onto the dirt, and looked around.

"Hey, there." She jumped and looked toward the voice to see Melissa seated in a rocking chair outside her front door. The other witch laughed. "Sorry, Lily. I didn't mean to scare you. Did they wake you?" Right on cue, the howls raised into the silence again and some of them ended in vicious snarls. It was much louder out there without the hum of the generator or four walls around her to dampen the sound. "Yeah, I can't sleep either when they do this."

"Have you been out here all night?"

"Naw. Only since about one o'clock when the neighbors started making all that racket." The older woman smirked. "What about your friend? Is he still sleeping through the noise?"

"Um…" Lily raised one bare foot to scrape the fine dirt off it against her other calf before she placed it back to the ground. "He stepped out, I guess. Did you see him—"

"He's not inside?" Melissa's hands clawed at the armrests of the rocking chair and her entire body tensed.

"No. He does that sometimes. You know. Goes out at night."

"Are you telling me he actually shifted into a wolf and went running around out here?" The woman's eyes were so wide, she thought she was about to start screaming in terror.

Her gaze shifted across the landscape in confusion. "If

that surprises you, I'd like to hear what your definition of a werewolf is."

"Shit." Melissa launched herself from the rocking chair and spun toward the house. "I thought you two were smart." She almost knocked her front door down with how forcefully she shoved it open and she disappeared inside.

"Okay, what's going on?" Lily hurried across the dirt toward the front door. "Melissa?"

The witch would have literally barreled over her if she'd been any closer to the doorway. She stormed outside again, slammed the door behind her, and shoved a pair of flipflops into the young woman's hands. "Put those on and get in."

"Hey—what is this? Where's Romeo?"

"Well, I have a fairly good idea," she grumbled. "Get in the truck, Lily."

She dropped the flipflops, shoved her feet into them, and scrambled across the loose dirt toward the passenger door of the gray pickup. The door handle stuck when she tried to open it, and Melissa had to lean across the cab to open it from the inside. The potions witch's door slammed shut, and Lily scrambled into the vehicle that had absolutely nothing in it but scattered trails of dirt and one of those dashboard bobbleheads. It was, she realized vaguely, a shark.

It took three attempts before the engine turned over, and the woman cursed the whole time. Finally, it rumbled to life and she backed up a few feet before she threw it into drive again with a sickening lurch and floored the gas pedal. Lily had to brace herself against the dashboard with both hands and as soon as she could, she shoved herself hastily back into the seat and buckled her seatbelt. Only then did she realize Melissa was off-roading at breakneck speed not through the community of adobe houses but behind her house, across the desert, and out into the middle of nowhere.

"Where are you going?" she shouted.

"Picking up after your reckless werewolf friend." The witch growled with evident irritation and slammed her palm on the steering wheel. "I said you'd be fine if you stayed in front of my house. Does he think he's invisible or something?"

"Romeo?"

"Oh, great. Now you're suddenly clueless too."

Lily shifted to face her and her head pounded as the truck hurtled over the small rocks and all the dry, prickly brush peppered across the desert. "Excuse me?"

The other witch did a double-take at her, then sniffed sharply and shook her head. "I'm sorry." She flexed her fingers over the steering wheel and grasped it tightly again. "This is simply far more trouble than I wanted." Her head whipped toward her companion again. "I'm only risking my neck like this because that boy's obviously important to you. And you're Greta's daughter."

"Well, I appreciate that." She swallowed and tried to see something—anything—in the blue semi-light. Everything remained black shadows against sprawling gray. "Now can you tell me what's going on?"

"Did you wonder why I build containment wards for this werewolf pack hiding me in their little village?"

"Well...yeah. But you said you don't ask about their business."

Melissa grunted. "That doesn't mean I don't know what it's for. I have to if I'm gonna whip up tailor-made magic that works." The woman's jaw clenched a few times. "This pack is into some nasty business, all right. The wards are meant to keep everything inside their arena. All magic. Any attempts to send communication. Astral projection's a bust too. The only thing that gets out is the sound."

Lily blinked. "Arena?"

"Yeah." The woman sighed and turned to meet her gaze while the cab rocked dangerously on the worst shock-absorbers ever and spewed a thick trail of dust behind them. "You've heard of cockfights, right? Dog fights?"

A cold weight pressed on her gut. "Yeah..."

"Well, these guys run their own fighting ring. Only it's not exactly with dogs."

She tried to keep breathing. "Melissa..."

"Werewolves, hon. They fight werewolves."

"What?"

"Exactly like your regular scummy fighting rings, they pit their best guys against whoever other packs bring in from all over Chihuahua, Durango, and Coahuila. I saw some come up from Jalisco a little while ago. They place their bets and throw their own into the ring. That's their business." The witch cleared her throat. "And they're not the kinda people who think twice about snatching a lone wolf off the side of the road and making a little extra money off the poor bastard."

"Oh, my God."

"Yeah. That's right. So, for whatever reason, it looks like your friend thought it was a good idea to sniff around in someone else's territory. And these guys do not have an open-door policy."

"Are you saying they took Romeo? To, what? Make him fight in a ring?"

"Yup."

"He wouldn't do that." Lily shook her head and forced herself to pry her aching fingers away from her own knees. She'd clenched them so tightly they'd probably left bruises. "He's not gonna fight another werewolf simply because someone tells him to."

"He will if they drug him and rough him up a little first. If that doesn't work, they'll threaten to target you the minute you drive your RV away from my front door and out into Mexico on your own."

It took three failed attempts before she finally swallowed the huge lump in her throat. "They can't do that."

"I'm very sure they did."

"No, I mean, it's ridiculously illegal. And...oh, my God."

"Does it look like there's anyone out here who's gonna care enough to stop 'em?" Melissa demanded. "Okay, yeah. Two people. You and me, Lily Antony. We're goin' in."

"Into what? If your containment wards are powerful enough to keep absolutely everything inside their—" She swallowed again. "Their arena...there's no way to get in from the outside, either."

"Correct." She buried her face in her hands and took a

few long, deep breaths. "Hey, look at me." The older woman chuckled. "Do I look worried? No, don't answer that. What I'm saying is that my containment wards do keep everything out but I built the damn things. And I'll tear 'em down too if I have to."

TWENTY-TWO

In less than ten minutes, Melissa brought her truck to a skidding halt in the desert valley. The sun had now begun to rise up over the eastern horizon and brought a golden haze to everything and a glow to a stand of trees beside the river less than half a mile away. It would've been beautiful if Lily wasn't already thinking about what would happen to Romeo—what might have already happened to him.

The witch shoved the driver's door open and didn't even bother to shut it behind her after she all but fell out. Lily struggled with her seatbelt, the door, and moving quickly enough across the arid ground in flipflops simply to catch up. The next wave of howling, barking, and snarling caught her completely off guard, and she whirled to search the empty landscape. "Why can't I see anything?" She glanced at her companion with wide eyes. "They sound like they're right here."

"They are." The potions witch stormed across the

reddening dirt and gestured with her hand like she threw something into the air. Immediately, her containment wards revealed themselves—various shades of red, all shimmering and wavering together in place to form a huge dome over the dry ground that had to be at least a mile wide. The very edge of it touched the river and the trees, and Lily could actually see the multiple layers of many different spells bound together in glistening colors. Dark shapes moved inside the dome.

"What are you doing?" she asked softly. *If I can hear them howling in there, they can probably hear me talking outside.*

"I'm shutting it down is what I'm doing." Melissa grunted, clenched her jaw, and her nostrils flared. Her hands moved through so many complicated gestures so rapidly that Lily couldn't pretend to follow the different spells. For all the woman's quirks, when it came down to it, she knew exactly what she was doing.

The next three minutes felt like three hours. Lily listened intently to the snarls and shouts from inside the warded area. She winced when a wolf yelped in pain, the sound immediately followed by one long, whistling whine. *Please, please, please, don't let that be him.*

In the next moment, the entire barrier flashed a bright white and the wards fell away as one to leave absolutely no trace of them behind. She summoned the most powerful defensive spell she knew and prepared for anything that would give her the chance to use it. Dozens of people turned casually to face the intruders but no one seemed too concerned about the appearance of only two witches. Most of them turned back within seconds to watch the current fight between a massive black wolf and a smaller gray one with a streak of blood along its flank. The combatants didn't pay them any attention, either.

A bald man in a denim jacket over a faded yellow t-shirt turned slowly from the fight to study the newcomers. One eyebrow raised when he recognized Melissa and he stepped hesitantly away from three women who stood beside him. Both of them—dark-skinned and black-haired—watched him leave. When they caught sight of Lily and Melissa, the closest one sneered and her teeth flashed dangerously in the dawn light. The other returned her focus to the fight.

"I thought you had no interest in the fights." The man stopped a few paces away from the witches. A hint of a Spanish accent laced his words but his English was perfect.

"I'm not here for the fights or the bets." Melissa stepped forward so they now stood only a foot apart. "You picked up the wrong stray, Hugo."

"Did I?"

Lily scanned the crowd gathered around the makeshift ring in the center—chain-link fencing erected in a circle on the dirt about fifteen feet in diameter. The wolves circled each other again and snarled and snapped their jaws. Romeo was a black wolf too, but he was nowhere near as large as the one in the ring.

"He's under my protection," the potions witch said, her voice low with warning. "Which you knew damn well when we arrived last night."

Hugo offered a small, humorless smile. "Then you should've tied him to your truck. If you want to protect your visitors, Melissa, I recommend you keep them on a short leash. This one found us after he'd followed our trail all the way out here. Tell me that doesn't sound like he wanted to participate in this."

"He had no idea what was going on," Lily said as she stepped toward them, her fists clenched. "You don't own the desert."

The bald man smirked. "I own this piece of it. Would you have preferred I gutted him for trespassing instead? Because this way, he still has the chance to fight his way out of this and prove his mettle in the ring."

"Romeo doesn't have to prove anything to anyone." She forced her glare away from the man to look through the crowd again. *Where is he?* "And you have no right to—"

"Lily." Melissa put a hand on her shoulder, calm but firm, and met her gaze sternly. "Go find him."

Hugo chuckled. "Yes. Go find him, Lily. And keep an eye on him until he finishes his first match. I really do look forward to seeing what he has to offer. He put up enough of a fight as it is. I hope it doesn't affect his performance. Which will be..." The man glanced over his shoulder at the fighting wolves as the black beast sank its teeth into its opponent's shoulder. "Fairly soon, I imagine."

She glared at the man, gritted her teeth, and left Melissa and the werewolf together. Something glinted on the man's denim jacket as she passed him, immediately below the right breast pocket—a silver pin in the shape of a heron, its wings spread wide and its neck curved in the telltale U shape. *Why the hell do I see a heron on a werewolf? You can come back to that later, Lily. Now, you have to find Romeo.*

The low hum of Melissa and Hugo's conversation followed her as she skirted the crowd but she couldn't hear what they said. She glanced at face after face and tried to ignore the snarls that issued from inside the fenced ring. Someone on her right barked a sharp, coarse laugh, and she whipped her head toward the sound. A man and a woman tapped their beer cans together and passed in front of her. When they were gone, she saw him.

"Oh, no." She broke into a run toward what had been the edge of Melissa's warded dome and the group of trees beside the river. The scrubby plants thinned and gave way to what could barely be considered grass. It was still dry and sharp enough to have cut his bare, bloody, dirt-stained feet. The rest of him wasn't much better off, either.

The clothes the werewolves had thrown on him were at least two sizes too big. A loose, dirty shirt hung off his shoulders, and the thin pants looked like they were about to fall off. The worst part was seeing him with his hands tied behind his back—and to the tree behind him—with what she assumed was the same metal chain looped in a crude collar around his neck. He stood well enough on his own, but his shoulders sagged and his head had lowered toward his chest.

She was almost there. "Romeo," she called. His head raised slowly at the sound of her voice, and she gasped. "Jesus." His left eye and upper lip were swollen and blood still dribbled from a huge gash on his brow. "What the hell did you do to him?" she shouted.

When the woman beside Romeo and the tree looked away from the fight, she resembled the two who'd stood with Hugo with the same dark-brown skin, straight black hair, and deep, cruel eyes. She also held the end of the heavy metal chain that secured her friend where he stood.

"Let go of—hey!"

Two huge Hispanic men appeared out of nowhere and stepped in front of her to block her path.

"Romeo!" She tried to step around one man but he shoved her back with his thickly muscled arm. "Don't touch me." She snarled defiance but both men merely stood there with their arms folded and stared at her. As she peered around the second man, Romeo's short-lived struggle to reach her ended abruptly. The woman beside him yanked viciously on the chain and he staggered with a low growl and would have fallen had he not been secured to the trunk. "Hey, I'm gonna get you out of here," she shouted.

The man on the left stepped sideways to block her view again. "*No es tu decisión.*"

That snippet of Spanish, she understood. "Not my decision? Well, I'm making it anyway." Lily stepped back and glared at the huge men. "Here's a decision for you. If you don't get out of my way, you're both gonna be in the dirt in about two seconds." She dropped the defense spell she'd been prepared to cast and summoned two handfuls of crackling red energy. "Move."

A round of cheers and brutal jeering rose behind her,

followed by one long, fierce howl of victory. Half the spectators raised their voices and although this series of frenzied howls were uttered by human throats, the sound itself was all wolf.

The man on her right thrust his hand toward her with incredible speed, but she dodged his grasp and delivered one of her crackling-red attack spells into his throat. He reeled and fell, choking. The second man snarled at her and his eyes flashed a werewolf's silver before a shift. She tilted her head challengingly at him. "Are you gonna be smarter than him?"

He hauled his shirt up over his head in response to reveal rippling muscle and a completely hairless torso. His threat of preparing to change forms didn't deter her, though.

"I don't want to fight wolves today." She sent her other attack spell into the center of the man's chest. He roared and staggered away, his eyes completely silver now, and his canines lengthened in his open mouth. Unfortunately, he didn't go down.

"*Oye! Que pasa?*" someone shouted behind her.

Lily tried to dart around the man again toward Romeo, but he snatched her wrist and gave her a sharp tug. She lashed out with a vicious sidekick, which would've been far more effective if she hadn't worn Melissa's flipflops. Her foot slipped out of the sandal when she made contact and while she'd kicked him hard enough in the ribs, he still didn't release her. She brought her forearm down on the inside of his elbow as hard as she could and launched another attack spell as a green sliver of light to slash against his gut. The man's grasp loosened and he grunted as he dropped to his knees with blood pouring down his belly.

She wasted no more time and sprinted the last few yards toward Romeo, losing the other flipflop in the process. When she finally reached him and caught him by the shoulders, his skin was slick with sweat and he swayed at the contact. "Hey. Hey, it's okay," she said.

His eyelids fluttered open, and his eyes rolled when he tried to look at her. "I can't...you..."

"I got you. We're getting you outta here."

The dark-haired woman still stood only a few feet away and jerked sharply on the chain's leash. Romeo uttered a strangled cry and sagged sideways with the tension it induced.

"Stop it!" Lily shouted. She didn't even think about the next spell. Somewhere in the back of her mind was the assurance that she'd already done it once and could do so again. Her hands clapped together sharply and when she pulled them apart, black smoke writhed between her palms. The woman's eyes widened.

"That's enough!" Hugo stormed toward them and gestured sharply at Romeo's guard. "*Déjalo.*" She sneered at the witch and ignored the command, whatever it was. "*Ahora,* Yasmin." With flaring nostrils, the woman turned her gaze on Hugo, scowled, and opened her hand. The chain fell with a jangle into the dirt.

"Lily." Melissa's gentle hand settled on her shoulder. "Let it go."

Despite the older woman's calm voice, it wasn't so easy for the younger woman to comply. She glared at the dark-haired woman and took a deep, shuddering breath. It took a long moment before the two inches of black smoke that swirled between her palms stilled. Her arms trembled as she pressed her hands together to force the power of a spell she really didn't understand into herself once again. It was as satisfying as having to sneeze and not being able to.

Melissa nodded and gave her a little nudge. Swallowing her anger, she leapt toward Romeo and lifted the chain that trailed from his neck. She had to loop it twice over his head to get it off and the release drew raspy sigh from his throat. The other end of the chain ran down his back and around his wrists before it attached to the tree behind him. His hands were frighteningly pale. An unraveling charm was easier and faster than trying to untangle the heavy restraints. The links broke in half and thumped in dozens of pieces at his feet. He grunted but didn't say a word.

"Get to the truck," the older witch said.

"Come on." Lily wrapped her arm around his waist and draped his arm over her shoulders. He stumbled and leaned almost all his weight on her while his head swayed and drooped toward his chest. "Woah. Easy." She guided him away from the wolves and the fighting ring toward the pickup, glaring at every werewolf who stared at her. Which was essentially everyone at this point. A few of them snarled at her but no one moved forward to reclaim their prisoner and no one else tried to stop her.

They passed a man who must have been six and a half feet tall. His bare chest and arms glistened with sweat and were streaked with dirt and blood. The teeth marks on his neck still trickled a little blood, even as the wound shrank and healed itself. A few yards away, a shorter but much more muscular man lay on his side in the dirt, completely naked and his eyes open and unseeing.

Lily looked away and focused on their vehicle. She tightened her hold around her friend's waist as he shuffled forward with her. *This is totally barbaric.*

"I assume you're prepared to make up for the loss," Hugo said and gazed calmly at Melissa. His eye twitched.

"Yeah, you can assume whatever you want. We both found a loophole in our agreement, pack master, so don't act like we're not splittin' the blame here fifty-fifty."

"I think I've already made reparations." He nodded at Lily and Romeo who had almost reached the truck.

The witch watched their stumbling progress for a moment before she puffed a breath out and smoothed her hair back from her forehead. "I'll double the monthly wolfsbane and I'll sound-proof the wards. It will be better for me too if I don't have to lose sleep listening to you slaughter each other." She scowled at him and spread her arms wide. "Is that reparation enough for ya?"

Hugo raised his eyebrows in consent. "Who is she?"

She shot him a warning glance. "Don't even think about it."

"I asked you a question."

"She's a witch, Hugo. What do you want me to say?"

"An incredibly powerful witch. And if I had to guess, she hasn't even fully realized it yet."

Melissa licked her lips and swallowed the bitterness in her mouth. "You don't know the half of it. And we're adding something else to this contract of ours. If you touch a hair on that girl's head, I will level your pueblo into the goddamn dirt. That includes after she leaves my house. You know damn well I can keep my eye on her as long as I want, so don't push it."

"Sure."

"Your word, Hugo." She drew a binding spell in the air, and the complex patterns appeared in striated, whirling orange light and rotated between them.

"You first, witch."

Melissa snorted and stuck her hand out. "Double wolfsbane and a sound-proof dome."

"I won't touch the girl." When she raised her eyebrows, Hugo cocked his head with a bitter smirk. "Or her friend."

"Done." The witch fought back a shudder when the pack master's hand clamped around her forearm but she waited for the binding to complete its purpose. The orange patterns within the spell's circle pulsed twice and the symbols dropped to settle over their clasped forearms. When they disappeared beneath Hugo's sun-tanned skin and her own slightly lighter flesh, a warm reminder of their pact spread through her arm. She released him and tried to turn away, but the man gripped her even harder and jerked her toward him.

"I don't appreciate what happened here, Melissa."

She glared at him and yanked her arm from his grip. "Yeah, me neither." She spun away and shoved her hands into her pockets, feeling the gazes of two full werewolf packs, a dozen unaffiliated spectators, and her own neighbors on her back.

"Why isn't he healing?" Lily jerked her hand away from Romeo's swollen eye when Melissa took them over a particularly rocky patch of semi-arid desert. He sat between them on the truck's bench seat, his head slumped forward. When the vehicle bounced, he uttered a muffled groan.

"I told you, they drugged him." The older woman took her eyes off the road long enough to see him slump forward. She pushed his shoulder gently back against the seat. "And the wolfsbane wore off too. A while ago, so it's a double whammy for him right now."

"How do they drug a werewolf into not healing?" Lily slid her arm across his chest to keep him upright and thought that dark, damp stain on someone else's shirt was probably blood.

"That is something I haven't gotten my hands on yet." Melissa looked thoughtful. "It would be useful in certain situations but those guys are definitely abusing it."

"Yeah, no kidding. Is he gonna be okay?"

"He will be when I'm done with him. If he pukes, lift his head up enough so he can breathe. Don't worry about the truck."

"Is he gonna puke?"

Romeo groaned again but didn't show any inclination to actually throw up, thank goodness.

"Almost there, kids."

The sun had barely poked up over the eastern horizon and the mountain range on that side of the Allende Valley. It almost blinded Lily as they raced across the dirt toward the werewolf compound of adobe houses where Melissa's home was tucked among them. The vehicle skidded to a stop, and the potions witch scrambled out to run around the front. She banged on the passenger door and Lily had to open it from the inside before she backed out and accepted the other woman's help to haul their patient out and manhandle him across the dusty yard. They managed to make it into the house, despite the fact that it was hard enough to walk through with all the junk everywhere even when they weren't trying to keep a drugged, beaten, six-foot-two werewolf from falling on his face.

Melissa snapped her fingers and a single wooden door appeared, suspended in mid-air beside the table in the middle of the room. She jerked it open and helped pull Romeo into an entirely different room. A huge pile of random papers, cartons, bottles, books, and clothes filled the middle of the room. The witch swiped her hand toward the wall and all of it rearranged itself into scattered piles there to reveal an actual bed.

"Go on and lay him down." She helped to lower him onto the mattress, and he groaned again as they supported him all the way onto his back. The woman ran the edge of her hand like a knife from the collar of the shirt Hugo's men had thrown on their prisoner down to the bottom hem. The fabric split in a neat line, and she jerked the sides down to expose three huge, circular bruises on his abdomen. "Bastards." She sighed, shook her head, and ran her hand lightly over his face. His eye had swollen shut now, but the gash on his forehead had almost stopped bleeding.

"All right. Come on."

"I'm not gonna leave him here—"

"The faster you get up to help me, girl, the quicker we can come back to help him. I dunno how much your mom taught you about potions, but you're gettin' another lesson right now. We need to be quick." Melissa rose from the bed and stalked out of the magically revealed bedroom.

Lily leaned over Romeo and ran her fingers lightly through his curls. Red-gold dirt spilled onto the pillow. "You're gonna be okay. You only need to hang in there a little longer." She left a gentle kiss on his un-swollen cheek.

His breath quickened. "There's no...can't..." He groaned again.

"Shh. It's okay."

"Lily!"

She caught his hand, gave it a quick squeeze, and stepped out into the main room of the home-turned-workshop.

"First thing." Melissa stood at the long bench spanning

the wall to Lily's left and sifted through the tub of labeled bottles. "Go grab four of the wolfsbane flowers. Make sure they're fully open and without any yellow left on the petals. Crush them in the bowl." Without looking, she pointed behind her to a stone mortar and pestle on the desk.

"Okay." She hurried to the potted plant hung from the ceiling and stared at the dark-purple flowers barely drooping over the sides. It was too high for her to see clearly which ones were open, let alone to check their coloring.

"Stool." The other woman pointed again without looking up.

She found the wooden step stool against the wall and beckoned it toward her with a minor levitation. It slid obediently across the wooden floor and stopped beneath the potted wolfsbane. She climbed onto the first step and sucked in a sharp breath through her teeth.

"Are you okay?"

"Yeah..." She raised her foot to study the bottom of it. At the time, she'd hardly felt the dry grass, prickly bushes, and rocky earth slicing into her bare feet but now, she'd left a smeared, bloody footprint on the wooden step stool and across the potion witch's floor. "I guess I got a little cut up." She stepped higher and examined the purple flowers in the planter. "I lost your flipflops too."

"Ha. You can make it up to me by working fast now and buying me a beer later." Melissa didn't pause in her work. She set a few labeled glass bottles out on the wooden counter and shoved everything out of the way with a forearm to make room for more work. "Forget the mess."

Ignoring her stinging feet, Lily found four of the right flowers in under a minute and plucked them from the stems. She stepped down and brought them to Melissa to be sure. "I don't wanna mess this up."

The potions witch leaned sideways to peer into her open palm. "You're Greta Antony's daughter. I don't think you could mess this up if you tried." With a nod, the witch returned to her own work, unscrewed the bottle lids, and focused intently on pouring a practiced amount of them into another metal bowl. "Oh. Here." She snatched another bottle and handed it to her. "Three tablespoons, you understand? Exactly."

Lily took the bottle and glanced at the workbench. "I don't have—" Melissa snapped her fingers and conjured a measuring spoon in her hand, which she held out to her temporary apprentice. "Thanks." She took it and moved to the mortar and pestle, dumped the flowers in, and began to crush them.

A massive groan came from the open doorway in the middle of the room.

"Keep going," Melissa said. "If we work fast enough, we can stop this thing."

"Stop what?"

With her back still turned toward her, the other woman shrugged. "Well, if he starts coughing up blood, we're in a whole different situation altogether."

A wheezing cough exploded from the room. The

potions witch whirled, glanced at the door, and nodded for Lily to go take a look. She dropped the pestle and dashed toward the suspended doorway. Romeo coughed again, took a gasping breath, and groaned and rolled his head to the side. "Please be okay," she whispered.

"Do you see blood?"

"No..."

"Then get out here."

She complied without argument and hastily crushed the last of the wolfsbane. By the time she'd added the last tablespoon of the clear liquid from the bottle labeled *Tlacote*, Melissa was at the desk beside her and balanced three different-sized metal bowls in her arms. She set each of them down and flipped a five-milliliter plastic syringe toward her assistant. "One of these in his mouth every ninety seconds, Lily. And count those seconds. Make sure he gets the whole thing every time. If he fights you, it'll suck, but you do what you have to do to get him to swallow. Eight of these. Ninety seconds. Twelve minutes. Set aside what's leftover. Go."

Lily scooped up the stone mortar and grabbed the syringe before she returned to the bedroom. Romeo wheezed constantly now. His closed eyelids fluttered rapidly and beads of sweat dribbled down his forehead. She sat on the bed beside him and filled the first syringe. The huge bruises on his stomach had doubled in size and looked more black than purple. His lips were way too pale, but they were parted enough for her to ease the syringe between them. When she pushed slowly on the plunger, she began to count.

He grunted a little at first but seemed more than grateful for what little liquid trickled into his mouth. She thought it was water, but it could have been anything.

Melissa's instructions had been explicit, and she was exact with her counting and with filling the syringe. The next two doses went down as easily as the first. On the fourth, another fit of coughing consumed him and she had to pull the dose away long enough that he wouldn't choke. He swallowed the rest of it and groaned. On the fifth dose, he closed his lips against the syringe.

"Come on. We have to do this." Her fingers brushed against his cheek, and although his brows flickered into a quick frown, he opened his mouth. Ninety seconds later, he turned his head away from her and mumbled his denial. "You have to." She had to turn his head toward her twice before she got the wolfsbane mixture in.

Halfway to the seventh dose, Romeo began to convulse and his chest heaved with sharp, jagged breaths. The black bruises on his stomach expanded and spread over his chest. The episode kept him from moving his head, so she took the opportunity to empty the seventh dose into his mouth, one milliliter at a time, and tried to time it with his choppy exhale so she didn't drown him with it. A moan gurgled from his throat, and when the syringe was empty, she bit her lip and ran her hand down his cheek again. "I'm sorry. One more."

When it was time for the last one, he had begun to shiver and his entire body glistened with sweat. Lily lifted the eighth syringe to his mouth and tried to wiggle it between his lips but his jaw was clenched shut and she couldn't get him to open it.

"Please," she whispered. "Romeo, you have to do this. It's gonna help, and you're gonna be okay. Open your mouth." A sharp grunt escaped him and the convulsions returned. Only this time, they were far more intense and his body bucked against the mattress. Either the drugs or his own tension had pinned his arms at his sides, but the rest of him lurched up and down. "Oh, my God. Melissa!"

Footsteps pounded into the bedroom and the other witch stopped for a moment with wide eyes before she rushed to the bedside. "Did you get it all in?" She tossed a corked vial onto the bed and stood at his head.

"Not yet. I tried. But then this started, and I can't—"

"How long ago?"

"What?"

"How many seconds since you were supposed to have that last dose in?"

Lily stood and tried to think. "I don't—"

"How long, Lily?"

"Nine! Nine seconds. Ten now."

"Okay." The older woman cradled the top of Romeo's head against the inside of her elbow, steadied her other arm on his chest, and grasped his chin. Her other hand clamped on his nose. He bucked constantly and now obviously tried to shake his head free. A strained gurgle rose in his throat and he tried to breathe through his clenched teeth but his lip was too swollen.

"What are you doing?" Lily shouted.

"When he opens his mouth, empty that whole thing inside. All at once."

"You're suffocating him!"

"Get over here and be ready."

She scrambled around the bed and crawled onto the other side to hold the syringe over Romeo's clenched mouth. He sounded like he was suffocating and tears welled in her eyes. She blinked them away to focus on the exact moment his mouth opened. When it did, he dragged in a raw, gasping breath and Lily shoved the plunger down with her other hand.

That did make him choke and he sputtered and his body shook violently when he half-swallowed and half-breathed the last dose. Melissa released him to prop him a little off the bed, helping the mixture down that way. The convulsions slowed, he coughed a few more times, and Lily's lower lip trembled at his next painful, desperate breath.

"Okay, now." The potions witch lowered him onto the bed. He still wheezed but he no longer thrashed and flailed. She looked at Lily and nodded. "Good job."

She wiped the tears angrily from her eyes with the back of her hand. "That could've killed him."

Melissa straightened from where she'd leaned over Romeo and shook her head. "No. But this definitely would if he didn't take all that wolfsbane. I'm certain there's such a thing as too much magic for a werewolf, especially when it's on the inside." She gestured to her own chest. "He needs everything you gave him to make it through what comes next."

Sighing, she closed her eyes and let her shoulders sag for a second. "What comes next?"

"My specialty." The woman grimaced and followed it with a tight smile. "A few of them, actually. Hand me that vial." Lily sat on her heels and snatched up the brown glass vial to hand it over. Melissa took it and turned to rummage through a pile of junk behind her. "Here." When she turned back, she held a pair of neoprene gloves.

"What are these for?"

"Fluids."

Lily glanced at Romeo, who was still breathing heavily but now lying still again. "You mean like blood and vomit?"

"Nope."

Swallowing, Lily took the gloves and pulled them on. "Have you done this before?"

"A few times." The other witch slipped her own gloves on with a snap, looked up, and met her companion's gaze. "I'm not technically a healer, Lily. I know they swear to something like that doctor's oath or whatever. Do no harm?" She sniffed. "Now, I won't say I go out of my way to do harm to anyone. But I don't really go out of my way to avoid it, either."

She blinked. "Please, say what you're trying to say."

Melissa cleared her throat and shrugged. "If I'd taken that oath as a healer, uh...some of them might say I'm about to break it."

"It's gonna hurt him."

"Well...it's not a bee sting."

Lily glanced at Romeo's face and the frown of discomfort that flickered over his features and took a deep breath. "Is there any other way to do this?"

"Maybe. But it'll be too late for him by the time I find out what it is and how to do it."

She bit her lip and smoothed the hair back from his sweaty forehead. Finally, she looked at her mom's old friend and nodded. "Do it."

TWENTY-FOUR

Melissa could probably have passed as a healer with her next action, which looked more like alchemy, anyway. She uncorked the vial in her gloved hand, tipped it, and emptied a glob of the thick, white, iridescent substance she'd whipped up while Lily forced wolfsbane down Romeo's unwilling throat. In silence, she coated the glove on one hand with it and smeared the goo onto the gash in his forehead, over his swollen black eye, and across his mangled cheek. Two fingers brushed the corner of his mouth and applied it to both lips, now that the bottom one had begun to swell too. Within seconds, the salve assumed a bluish color and shimmered on his skin without any change of the lighting in the room.

The potions witch dumped a much larger amount into her hand again and held the vial toward Lily. "Close it." She did as she was told while her companion rubbed her gloved hands together. The smell of days-curdled milk filled the bedroom, and she leaned away with flared nostrils. "It's okay to breathe through your mouth." Melissa glanced at her and smirked. "You get used to it."

When her gloves were sufficiently coated, she gazed at the werewolf's torso and took a deep breath. His entire abdomen was one massive bruise now. "Jesus, that's nasty. I've never seen it get this far."

"What's happening?"

"That's the drug part—whatever it is they use. Hugo uses it on his own fighters before a bout. It keeps the wolves from healing and raises the stakes. He puts a little more down their throats if he's thrown the match. Unfortunately, he won't let me make an antidote 'cause that would simply be reverse-engineering what he's given them anyway. But I told him how to get the drug out afterward. There's definitely a weakening curse in there, but I haven't—"

"Hugo can use magic, too?"

"What? No, of course not. He has a few other magicals working for him." The woman shook her head. "Werewolves using magic. That's never gonna happen."

"I've seen it."

"What?"

Lily nodded and pursed her lips. "That's a long story. And maybe you should—"

Melissa looked at Romeo's torso again and nodded. "Yep. Sorry. It surprised me how advanced it is, that's all. Okay." She puffed out a breath, rolled her shoulders back, and smeared the white substance she'd created all over his stomach. His hips and ribcage had turned the same purple-black now, and Lily couldn't tell where the original bruises were anymore. The witch covered all of it and pressed her hand once against the center of his chest to leave a glistening white handprint there. "I'm sure you know this, but I gotta put it out there. If you interrupt me, he's as good as gone. Got it?"

"Yeah."

"Good." She removed her gloves, yanked them inside out, and tossed them over her shoulder and snapped her fingers. They vanished and she held her hands over Romeo's body and watched intently. When the white substance took on the same bluish tint, she wiggled her fingers, took a deep breath, and closed her eyes.

The woman's breath came out again in one long, low, shushing exhale. The tips of her fingers glowed a muddled green. She balled her hands into fists, opened them again, and breathed in the same way. The process was repeated a few times and with each breath, the light at her fingertips grew brighter and brighter. Her lips moved with an incantation barely above a whisper. Lily couldn't hear any of it.

Romeo's eyelids fluttered rapidly and a few short moans escaped his open mouth. Melissa closed and opened her hands, breathed out again, and the substance covering his wounds began to glow too. But now, it was a dark, fiery-looking red and grew brighter with every second. Lily smelled burnt hair as the glowing liquid singed his eyebrow. It started to bubble on his skin and the smell of burnt hair was joined by that of barbeque.

"Oh, my God." She swallowed, but she couldn't bring herself to look away from what was happening. Half of his face, his stomach from immediately below his chest to his hips, and the handprint in the center of his chest all bubbled now and glowed a fiery-orange spread a red heat across his skin. His breath came rougher and faster and he groaned in unbearable pain.

Melissa opened her eyes, drew her hands back, and sucked in a breath. "Lily, hand me a rag or something."

She leapt off the bed to look through the piles of junk on the floor. "Um...there's no... What about a pillowcase?"

"Perfect." The woman gestured impatiently for the dark-purple pillowcase and she tossed it over the bed before she climbed beside Romeo despite the fact that she could hear his skin sizzling. Thin trails of smoke rose from his body, and his moans were one constant stream of voiced agony. "Almost there..." With the pillowcase in her right hand, Melissa stared at the handprint on his chest and hovered over him with wide eyes like she preparing to snatch a fish out of water with her bare hands.

The air pressure around them shifted, and Lily's ears popped. Goosebumps trailed down her bare arms and legs and all the salve burning through his body flashed a bright light at once.

In the same second, the older witch raised her left arm and arced her hand to slap the handprint, and Romeo screamed.

Every muscle in his body tensed and the veins in his temple throbbed dangerously, and still, he screamed. Melissa grimaced with the effort of drawing this much magic and poison out of him at the same time and braced herself against the mattress. Her shoulder trembled as she raised her hand from his chest—which was incredibly hard to do because the poison had now latched onto her palm and clung to them both.

Lily's mouth dropped open when she saw the flailing, black-green tendrils rise out of Romeo's body and flick toward Melissa's palm. The air filled with static, and she couldn't stop her teeth from chattering. His continuous scream finally made her clamp her gloved hands over her ears.

With a shout, the witch jerked her arm away and ripped the writhing, flapping blackness completely out. His scream cut off. Immediately, she clamped the pillowcase over her hand. "Shit, that burns." She casually wiped it all off like she'd finished washing dishes and flung the pillowcase over her shoulder with another snap of her fingers. The linen and the poisoned curse on it both disappeared.

The static faded from the air. Lily's skin no longer tingled. Romeo's skin had stopped bubbling and all the redness was gone. Melissa's potion still remained but it had returned to its bluish hue.

Lily leaned back on the bed and stared at him. "What was that?"

"Whatever keeps a magical from doing what they were made to do. He'll heal himself now." Melissa shrugged. "The rest isn't dangerous. It won't hurt him, either. But if you're squeamish—"

"I'm not going anywhere."

The other witch met her gaze and nodded. "Okay, then. I'll be right back." She left the room, and Lily stared at her friend's face. He was breathing evenly, his frown completely gone and his features seemed as peaceful as they could with all the swelling. His color seemed to have improved too.

"Okay. It looks like this worked. I am so sorry you had to go through that."

Melissa returned, wearing a new pair of gloves and carrying two more metal bowls and a package of baby wipes. She chuckled at Lily's confusion. "Don't worry. We're playin' nurse now for a few minutes. We gotta clean it all up." She handed her a bowl and set the wipes at the foot of the bed beside his bare feet.

"Clean what, exactly?"

The other witch nodded at the patient. What looked like pus oozed from the cut in his eyebrow and his swollen eye and bruised cheek, only it was a bright, noxious green. It dribbled from the corner of his mouth and his puffy lips.

"What is that?"

"That's what Hugo feeds his wolves with the curse. Mostly, I think, he gives it to the ones who don't actually wanna step into the ring." The green slime rose from the skin on Romeo's belly and chest like beading drops of sweat and more of it pushed itself out of him every second. "Shall we?" Melissa took a wipe, raised an eyebrow at her companion, and set to work wiping the nasty stuff off him.

Lily took her own wipe and focused on his face. She dabbed gingerly at his swollen flesh and tried not to hurt him and get as much of the green stuff off as she could. It didn't hurt him at all, apparently. He could have been asleep given how little he reacted to the cleaning process. When the wipes were soiled, they tossed them into the metal bowls. The green ooze simply kept coming. Still, the bruising faded quickly and the battered flesh on his face regained its normal shape with every new layer of bright green gunk she wiped away.

By the time it stopped, his body had healed the remainder of his wounds on its own and their metal bowls almost overflowed with green-stained baby wipes. Melissa collected the bowls and turned to open a cabinet built into the wall. She put both inside and closed the door.

"That's not really a cabinet, is it?" Lily asked.

"No, not really." They stripped their gloves off, and the older witch added both sets to the cabinet as well, which was empty when she opened the door and would be empty again once she had closed it. When she turned again, Lily had covered her eyes with her hand. "Are you okay?"

"Yeah. I only... I think I need some air." She lowered her hand. "Is he gonna be okay?"

"He's totally out of the woods now, Lily. After he rests for a while, you'll both forget all about it."

"I doubt that." She took his hand—which was warm and pink again—and kissed the back of it before she crawled backward off the bed and headed through the suspended door. "I really need some air." She went all the way through Melissa's cluttered house and outside into the morning sunshine. The sun was already high in the sky, and the temperature had followed suit. The chill that had crept slowly down her spine faded. She slumped into the rocking chair outside the door, draped her hands over the armrests, and closed her eyes.

The morning seemed too quiet for what she'd just been

through. She opened her eyes when an insect scuttled along the dirt in front of her and the tips of the scrubby bushes dotting the ground trembled in a light breeze. *I can't believe this day happened.*

"Here." Melissa stepped outside, closed the door behind her, and set a large plastic tub of hot water on the ground beside her feet. "Pick your feet up, kid." When she obeyed, she slid the tub to where they'd been and nodded.

The minute Lily's toes touched the water, the burning sting in her feet she'd ignored for what felt like hours faded away into nothing. It smelled like lavender and honey and something a little astringent. She sighed and dropped her head back against the rocking chair. "Thanks."

"Yeah, that'll set you right." The woman sat in the dirt beside the rocking chair, drew her feet close, and draped her forearms over her bent knees. "He's gonna be fine. And you did all right."

Lily snorted. "If you say so."

"No, really. Most people walking into a werewolf den like that would turn around and hightail it outta there. You didn't even flinch. I know people compare bravery and stupidity all the time, but you're definitely not stupid. And you know how to fight, which is something I never quite learned. I guess your mom taught you that too, huh?"

"Yep."

"Well, we all have our strengths. I fight in the potions lab, as it were. You weren't too bad at that, either."

She laughed dryly. "I have no idea what we did in there."

"We saved him is what we did."

"I should've thanked you for that first." She opened her eyes and looked at Melissa, who smirked at her.

"Hey, I know how good a healing foot bath can be. Don't worry about it." The woman sniffed and looked across the dry ground where the morning sun cast long shadows behind the other buildings of her new neighborhood in Mexico.

"Are you gonna be...in trouble after helping us?"

"What? Ha." Melissa shook her head. "I'm always in trouble with one thing or another. If you're askin' will I have to fight Hugo and his pack off me after this, the answer's no. I give them too much of what they need for them to punish me. Or to try, at least. And for now, they're still the safest hiding place I have. Don't worry about me, Lily. I've helped many people out of much worse than what Romeo got himself into. And I've talked myself out of more trouble than I like to admit." She chuckled, and they sat there for a few more minutes and simply let the morning pass them by.

Lily yawned. "Jeeze. Sorry."

"That's silly. You know what? You should get some rest. We still have a few hours of wait time before your mom's deposit is ready to show itself. Go on inside, if you want. You have a nice bed and a warm body waiting in there for you if you want 'em. I'm not goin' anywhere."

She studied the woman, who for the first time, looked older than her mid-forties which she had to be if she was around Greta Antony's age. "Yeah. That sounds good, actually. And it's not like there's really anything else to do right now, huh?"

"Nope. Now we merely let the rest of the world work itself out."

Lily raised her feet from the tub of hot water and glanced at the soles. All the cuts and scrapes were gone. "That's amazing."

Melissa winked. "You're welcome."

Smiling through her exhaustion, she stood and walked inside the house. The suspended door to the extra bedroom was still open but she shut it behind her. The overhead light turned off on its own, and she walked around the bed before she crawled onto the comforter beside Romeo. He still lay on his back, his arms down by his side, and exhaled tiny snores every few breaths. She stretched out on her side, took his hand in both of hers, and stared at his profile until she dropped into sleep.

TWENTY-FIVE

Lily had no idea what time it was or how long she'd slept when she woke again. When the entire debacle of that morning came back to her, she jolted and sat up. "Oh, thank God." Although the light was still off and there were no windows, it wasn't completely dark. Romeo was clearly still in the bed beside her, and he hadn't moved an inch since she'd laid down for a little more rest. "I'm so glad you're still here," she whispered and brushed his hair back from his forehead.

He stirred on the bed, blinked his eyes open, and focused on her face. "Hey." He gave her a lazy smile.

"Hey." She leaned over him to kiss the corner of his mouth, which was completely healed.

His hand brushed against her thigh but he tensed and drew back to look at her. "What's wrong?"

"Nothing. How're you feeling?"

"Uh...weird."

She laughed. "That basically sums it up, although it might be an understatement—woah. Take it easy."

Romeo propped himself up on his elbows and raised an eyebrow. "I'm okay. It's not like I—" He stopped when he noticed the room they were in. "This isn't the Winnie."

"Nope."

He stared at her. "Why aren't we in the Winnie?"

Lily took a deep breath and bit her lip. "What's the last thing you remember?"

It took a minute for him to sort through the jumble of his memories. "I was up in the middle of the night. I think all the...howling woke me up. You were sleeping through it, so I thought I'd go out and see what the big deal was. I shifted and went for a run in the—" His mouth dropped open, and his eyes widened. "Lily, I knew something wasn't right here with these wolves. I felt it. I could smell it. I only... I didn't know what it was. I didn't know what they were doing. They came out of nowhere and—"

"Hey, it's okay." She rubbed his back gently. "It's okay. Melissa and I found you and brought you back here."

"Yeah, where is here?"

"Oh. Uh, she has a disappearing door into an extra bedroom."

Romeo gurgled a laugh. "Of course she does."

"She's actually incredible. The whole time, she kept saying she wasn't a healer but without her, I don't...I don't think you would've made it."

"What happened?"

She hesitated as she considered what to tell him and finally settled on all of it in abridged form. "Well, you had the crap beaten outta you. Then, you were curse-poisoned and drugged. The pack master here named Hugo had you chained to a tree and was gonna make you fight in a ring—as a wolf. Melissa tore the wards down, I kicked a few asses, and we brought you back here to heal you. Now, you're healed." She smiled, but it fell completely flat.

"Lily?"

"Yeah."

"I remember being attacked by three wolves at the same time. That's it. Out of...oh, I dunno, some kind of morbid curiosity, can you run me through the long version too?"

For the first time since she'd woken up at 4:00 that morning, she felt complete relief. "Yes. The long version. You're not gonna believe this."

"I'm on a bed in a room I've never seen before, half-naked and wearing someone else's pants. I have no reason not to believe you."

Laughing, she nodded, scooched closer to him against the pillows, and told him everything.

"So now, I think the next step is to check out whatever my mom left in four-fifty-two."

"Do you still think it's in Melissa's vault?"

Lily tucked her hair behind her ear and smiled. "You know, I was admittedly a little skeptical of her and what she's doing here at first. But she seriously pulled through for you. For us. I watched her work powerful magic,

Romeo. If she says that bowl of red slop with the keychain in it is gonna open my mom's box of valuables, I believe her."

He chuckled. "Okay. It's gotta be after ten, right?" To punctuate the question, his stomach emitted a huge, gurgling roar. "I'm starving."

"Yeah, me too. I don't have my phone with me, so..." She shrugged. "Let's go have a look at what we have. Do you think you can walk?"

"Lily, I feel great. Really. You don't have to keep asking."

"Okay." She slipped off her side of the bed and he stood at the same time. "I half carried you out of a fighting pit and you could barely hold yourself up in the truck, so I'm only trying to be—" She stopped when she saw his chest.

"What?"

"Uh..."

"Is there something on my—aw, what the hell?" He looked at his chest and rubbed the skin there. "What is this?" His fingers poked and prodded the mark there like he could erase it.

"That...looks like a new scar."

"In the shape of a hand, Lily. I thought you said everything went back to normal after Melissa's healing."

"She's not actually a healer—"

"Or whatever. Did she...brand me or something?"

She stepped slowly toward him. "I don't think it was on purpose."

"No, of course not. That would make this totally weird."

Snorting and trying hard not to laugh, she crossed the room and stood in front of him to study the thin but definitely existent lines of Melissa's handprint now scarred into his chest. She bit her lip and raised her own left hand, which fit perfectly over the new mark. "Well, hey." His heart raced beneath her palm. "Would it be any better if you thought of it as a reminder? A good one, I mean. That you almost died"—he laughed in disbelief—"but you didn't. Because I force-fed you wolfsbane and helped a friend remove a curse from literally inside your body."

Romeo held her gaze and covered her hand that rested on his chest with both of his own. "Maybe a little better." Lily grinned. "But only a tiny bit better. A sliver, really. It's barely even there."

"Better is better, right?"

He pulled her closer and kissed her, wrapped his arms around her, and buried his face in the curve of her neck and shoulder. She hugged him in return and sighed. "Thank you," he muttered and hooked his chin over her shoulder. "I'm sorry you had to do any of it but thank you."

She spread her hands across his bare back and couldn't hold enough of him at the same time. "Always."

When he released her, he almost looked at his chest again but shook his head. "Let's go see what your mom left with Melissa. Let's get it and see where it takes us next. And I really want to get back into my own clothes."

Lily chuckled. "That sounds good." She slipped her hand into his and turned the knob of the disappearing door. He was completely surprised to step out into the center of the woman's house. She stopped to pull the door closed behind her, and he whirled to study the thing suspended by magic and nothing else.

"No kiddin'."

"Yeah, I didn't expect it, either. Melissa?"

A loud snore came in reply, followed by a gasp. Melissa's disheveled brown hair appeared from behind a stack of more junk against the back wall. "What? What's in the... Oh. Oh. Mornin'." She ruffled her hair a little and offered a groggy smile. "Well don't you look all back up on your feet." With a grunt, the witch pushed herself to her feet and ignored the shower of loose papers and single shoes that toppled around her.

Lily and Romeo shared a glance, and she bit her lip to restrain her laughter.

"Lily told me what you did," he said. "Thank you."

"Oh, yeah. Yeah, sure." Melissa sniffed and blinked her wide eyes back into focus. She stepped toward them, studied him carefully, and paused. "Next time a witch tells you you're safe as long as you stay right outside her house, I highly suggest you take that literally." He took a deep breath like he was about to say something but nodded instead. "Well, it's kinda hard for you to forget that lesson now, isn't it?" She gestured to her own chest. "I didn't mean anything by it, kid. Honestly. But it's...it's nice..." Her words were cut short by a sharp burst of laughter. "It's nice to see I've left a mark somewhere in this world!" She threw back her head and roared with laughter, kicked out at the pile of stuff beside her, and launched some of it against the back wall.

"Should I go get changed first?" he muttered.

"Well, that's up to you." Lily smirked when he raised his eyebrows and turned to step out of the house for a few minutes. By the time Melissa had calmed after her hilarity, he was already in the Winnie.

"Aw, where'd he go?" The potions witch wiped her eyes, still chuckling, and headed toward the far corner where the workbench met the back wall. "Did I scare him away?"

"He wants his own clothes," Lily said.

"Well, I can't blame him for that." The woman's laughter finally ceased and she bent under the workbench to retrieve the large metal bowl in which she'd summoned four-fifty-two from her vault. She brought it to the desk in the center of the room, set it down, and peered inside before she stepped back.

The younger woman peered into the bowl, but it was still merely a slightly rippling mixture of thick red liquid. "Did we miss something?"

"Hey, you like being a comedian, huh?" Melissa winked. "No. We didn't miss something. I thought I'd wait for Romeo to get his troublemaking butt in here first, seeing as he missed all the other excitement."

Lily smirked. Before she could respond, the front door opened and Romeo stepped inside, dressed in shorts and a t-shirt. He scratched his chest absently. She pressed her lips together and turned back toward the bowl.

"Just in time," Melissa declared.

"Did we get it?" He stopped beside Lily in front of the desk and frowned at the bowl. "That looks like a no."

"We're not finished yet, thank you very much." The woman shook her head in mock indignation and she raised her hand, poised for another signature snap of her fingers. "Are you ready for this?"

"Uh, I think we've waited long enough," Lily said.

"I'll agree with you there." The potions witch gazed into the bowl, raised her fingers a little higher, snapped them, and opened her palm. A wooden box materialized in her hand, and she grunted beneath the surprising weight and size of it. The box almost slipped out and onto the floor, but she managed to catch it with a chuckle and set it gently on the table.

It was a foot long and made of thick, heavy wood with a gold hinge on one side and a gold clasp on the other. On the lid was an etched design of a lily flower in the same style they'd found inside the trunk in the invisible cabin in Canada. "Now's as good a time as any," Lily said and stretched her hand to the clasp.

"Oh. Look who's a little overconfident."

"What?" She jerked her hand back. "You said it would absolutely work."

Melissa shrugged and the corners of her mouth turned down with feigned indifference. "If it doesn't, that means you aren't really who you say you are, Lily Antony."

"What?"

The older witch raised her eyebrow and huffed a wheezing laugh. "That's so much fun. Messin' with you. Go ahead. It'll work."

She rolled her eyes with an exasperated smirk and undid the clasp on the box. Although she held her breath as she did so, nothing happened. "Well, I guess that's a good sign." She opened the lid and peered inside. It contained three things, exactly like the last clues her mom left for her. She retrieved the scrap of paper first and a little of the tense anticipation lifted when she recognized the handwriting.

'SO HERE YOU ARE AGAIN, *sweets, reading my little notes. I'm so proud of you. Don't ever forget how deeply the roots of loyalty, trust, and unending friendships truly stretch into the soil of our lives. These things will always be there for you if you open yourself to them. The only chains that truly bind us in life are the ones we forge ourselves. And sometimes, the places that seem the safest turn out to be far more dangerous than we ever imagined. You know how to tell the difference.'*

THIS NOTE WASN'T SIGNED EITHER, but it was definitely her mom's handwriting. Lily felt Romeo's gaze on her, so she handed him the note to read and reached into the box for the second item. There was another small purse this time too, and she picked that up next because she knew what it was. It almost overflowed with even more gold coins. "There's gotta be more in here than the last one."

"More what?" Melissa asked and tried not to seem too curious.

"Gold," Romeo said and wiggled his eyebrows although he still read Greta Antony's note.

"That little..." The potions witch shook her head and laugh. "Of course she left actual gold in a magical deposit box."

"And this." Lily removed the last item in the wooden box and had to hold it in both hands because it was so heavy. "What the heck is this?" The stone was the same size and shape as a mason jar and tinted a jade-green but wasn't made of jade. A face was carved into the front below the smoothly rounded head—two black eyes above a black mouth open in an 'o.' "It kinda gives me the creeps."

"Well, it shouldn't." The other woman peered across the desk and held her hand out. "Can I see?"

"Sure." Lily placed the stone in her palm and Melissa held it with two hands as well as she turned it a few times to study it.

"Yeah, I've seen these before. They're everywhere at this...healing temple in Guatemala. Ichacál, I think it's called. They're supposed to be good-luck charms or something. Even before I moved here, I never heard of these showing up anywhere else but in that temple." She handed the stone back and sniffed.

"Then that's where we need to go." Lily looked at Romeo. "At least we won't have to drive in the complete opposite direction again."

He snorted. "Lily, I'd drive in circles with you if that's what we had to do."

"Aw, that's sweet. I'd puke if we drove in circles." She

laughed and set the stone in her mom's wooden box. "So let's take that one completely off the table, huh?"

"Wait a minute. Am I missing something, here?" Melissa glanced at each of them and frowned. "Why does a rock in a box mean you two have to drive all the way to Guatemala now?"

Lily took a deep breath. "Should we tell her?"

Romeo shrugged. "Well, she did leave her literal mark on me. We might as well return the favor."

"Yeah, but ours won't be literal—"

"I'm standing right here." The other woman slapped her hands on the table and leaned toward them. "What is going on?"

Lily met Romeo's gaze, then nodded toward the older witch. He handed Melissa the scrap of paper with the note from Greta Antony, and they stood there in silence while she read it.

TWENTY-SIX

It couldn't have taken anyone longer than twenty seconds to read that relatively short note but Melissa stared at the scrap of paper in her hands for a full minute. Finally, she frowned and looked at Lily. "What is this?"

"A note from my mom."

When the potions witch looked at Romeo, he merely nodded.

"You realize she wrote this for you at least three years ago, yeah?"

"Yep."

"And you understand how incredibly weird it is to see all these things in this note, right? Chains. Loyalty. Safe places holding danger."

She nodded. "Yep."

Melissa's eyes widened, and she snorted. "Greta could've written this two hours ago." She smoothed her tousled hair from her face and puffed her cheeks. "Unbelievable."

"Okay…" Lily leaned toward Romeo. "Now, I'm starting to think our reactions were a little mild."

"She's your mom," he said. "Why would you be surprised by anything she does?"

"Yeah, it is fairly rare."

"I still don't get it." Melissa handed the note to Lily, who put it into the box. "Why are you going anywhere else but home after this?"

"You're literally only the third person I've told about this," she said. "And I need you to promise first that you won't tell anyone. Not until I have more proof."

The older witch shrugged. "If you want me to pull up a binding vow or—"

"Nope. No thanks." She laughed wryly. "I'm not a big fan of those. And I trust you enough to keep your promise anyway. If you make it."

"Of course I promise, Lily."

"Thank you." She tucked the purse of gold coins into the wooden box as well, closed the lid, and latched it again. With her hands resting on the wood, she looked at Melissa and drew a deep breath. "I don't think my mom's actually dead."

The woman coughed and stared at the box. "I believe that'll require more of an explanation."

"Yeah, I know." Lily looked at Romeo. "We have time, right?"

"Enough for this. As far as I know."

"Okay. Maybe we should sit for this."

Melissa finally met her gaze and one of the woman's eyes twitched. "Sure. Do you two like beef jerky?"

"Um..." Lily chuckled.

"It's simply that I'm starving and I have a crapload of beef jerky. And tamales. I'll whip up breakfast while you whip up a story."

"Deal," Romeo said before Lily had the chance to answer. She simply sighed and opened her mouth to ask where she could find chairs. Melissa beat her to it and summoned three rickety seats around the desk as she stared with wide blue eyes at Greta's wooden box on the table. After a hasty shake of her head, she turned to rummage through the cabinets beside the shelf along the back wall and gestured for Lily to talk.

NOTHING WAS LEFT out of Lily's story. She went over everything for Melissa's benefit, starting with the witch in the gray suit who'd tried to assassinate her in broad daylight at home in Charleston. Romeo pitched in with a few extra details here and there, and the woman didn't say a word until Lily ended with, "Then we met you at that bar down the road, and here we are." She ripped off another chunk of beef jerky between her teeth and told herself to chew slowly. Her jaw was already sore from talking.

The potions witch nodded and fixed her gaze on Lily. "Let me see the necklace she left you."

"Oh. Sure. It's right here." She reached to the clasp at the back of her neck.

"No, don't...don't take it off." The woman scooted her

chair closer and scooped up the tiny framed mirror hanging from the chain at her throat. "How the hell did she get her hands on one of these?"

"What is it?" she asked.

Melissa released the necklace, leaned back in her chair, and nodded. "You have a legit revocation amulet around your neck, girl. That thing's as close to time travel as any witch will ever get."

"Time travel." Romeo raised an eyebrow.

"That amulet..." The older witch puffed her cheeks in disbelief. "It reverses the most recent, most powerful magic cast around the wearer. Then, it pulls the plug on that specific spell or charm or what have you."

"Huh?"

"What it reverses, it also cancels out, right? That same use of magic can't be repeated again for a long time afterward. I'm not exactly sure how long, but I'm willing to bet it's at least a week."

"Oh." She fingered the framed mirror at her throat. "Oh. That finally makes sense."

"Not to all of us, Lil."

"Right. Sorry. Hey, when you were shot outside that cabin, I did actually think it killed you."

"Ha!" Melissa immediately clamped a hand over her mouth, drew her fingers across her lips, and pretended to zip it.

"And I thought this brought you back to life at first. I know. It's kinda ridiculous."

"Nope." He caught her hand. Melissa sighed, folded her arms, and smiled at them.

"Well, obviously, it didn't do that." Lily bit her lip. "The club owner and his bouncers or whatever found us really quickly at the cabin. And we never heard them coming. If they teleported to that exact place—which would've been easy for the club owner, seeing as I'm reasonably sure it was his cabin—that would explain everything. None of the spells I used against him were anywhere near as powerful as a teleport. That's what I undid when I used the mirror, isn't it?"

The other woman tilted her head with a noncommittal shrug. "It's entirely possible."

"They didn't suddenly disappear. I sent them back to wherever they came from. They didn't try again, either, because the spell they'd used for it was...what? Frozen by the mirror."

"Temporarily suspended." The potions witch sniggered.

"Woah." Romeo folded his arms and stared at Lily's necklace. "That's actually a really great first magical item for your mom to leave you."

Melissa hummed in agreement. "Yes, it is."

"Oh, man. I almost forgot." Lily rubbed her face. "That werewolf—Hugo. He had a pin on his jacket. It was the same heron shape from the business card and painted on the back wall through the black door."

He cleared his throat. "Why would a screwed-up pack master and a magical club-owner have the same bird featured in their businesses?"

"Weird, right? Melissa, do you know anything about it?"

She shook her head. "That heron doesn't mean anything to me, Lily. Sorry. The most I know about Hugo is that he used to travel all over the world to recruit new wolf fighters for the ring. He made an impressive career out of it—monetarily only, mind you. It's not impossible that he might have visited this circus party in Montreal. He likes to fancy himself retired now, I think."

"Hey, that club also had a werewolf who could practice magic, remember?" Lily turned to Romeo and she straightened in his chair.

"Yeah, that threw me off."

"Wait, I recall that you mentioned that before." Melissa sniffed and leaned forward. "You saw a werewolf practicing magic? Like casting spells and everything?"

"Like I said." He gestured vaguely with his hands as if to indicate his own confusion. "It totally threw me off."

"They might have been using wolfsbane in Canada," Lily suggested.

"I was thinkin' the same thing. But it means that werewolf would've had to practice everything he knew without actually using magic between his doses. And I have no idea how long the flower stays in effect if it's used on a regular basis like that."

"They might be connected but I have no idea how."

"Well, we can come back to that one eventually." Melissa chuckled. "At least now, I'll know what to do if I see any other heron-looking things around here."

"What's that?"

"I'll call you two. It'll be nice to defer to someone with a little more experience in this matter than me."

"Yeah. Very little."

"Hey, it's better than nothing," Romeo said with a wink. "And now, we get to go to Guatemala.

MELISSA WAS able to give them the relative location of the Ichacál healing temple, which Romeo promptly looked up on his phone. "Oh, it's a good thing I have Wi-Fi out here, huh?" The potions witch laughed. "Sorry I don't have much else to send with you on your way."

"Don't apologize for anything." Lily shook her head and stopped in front of the Winnie's side door. "You've already given us more than enough." She opened her arms —her mom's wooden box placed safely on the step of the vehicle—and caught Melissa in a tight, long hug. The older witch tensed for a minute, then lifted her hands to pat Lily's back gently. "Thank you so much. For everything."

"I don't think there's a thing I wouldn't do for you, Lily. If it's in my power, that is. I loved your mom. Or maybe still do, right? That is if you find out where she is and it turns out the whole magical world's pickin' up someone else's dirty lie."

"That's exactly what I'm trying to find out. And tear down, whatever it takes."

Melissa cupped Lily's cheek and narrowed her eyes. "Good. Don't you lose that fire, girl. It'll light your way right to her." She nodded. "And *you*." The woman turned to Romeo and shook a finger at him. "I'm serious about taking the rules seriously, kid. Not all of them, of course.

Never all of them." She placed her hand on his chest and looked at him. Romeo lowered his head slowly to look at her hand, which she had placed over his new scar in the exact position. The woman threw her head back and laughed heartily before she shoved him away again. "I'll try to avoid that little side effect in the future."

He smirked and spread his arms. "And I'll follow the rules. Only the ones that apply to me, though." He stepped forward and hugged her too, which made her even more awkwardly uncomfortable than Lily's hug.

When he released her, she stepped back and threw her hands up. "I have never been hugged so much in one day. I'm gonna...go work on something." She pointed at him and turned toward her house. "Lily."

"Yeah."

"You have my number. Call me if you need anything. And definitely call me if you find her."

"When I find her." Grinning, she nodded and turned to open the Winnie's side door. Romeo climbed into it after her, followed by Melissa's fading laughter before she disappeared inside her home.

TWENTY-SEVEN

Lily insisted on driving, at least for the first leg of their trip farther south to Guatemala. "Look, you went through the wringer, okay? I don't think being behind the wheel is the best thing for you right now."

"Oh..." Romeo leaned back in the passenger seat and raised his legs. "So you want me to sit back, relax, and kick my...feet..." She burst out laughing when his long legs simply took up too much room. "Yeah, okay. I can't even get my feet on the dash. But you get the point."

"If we're talking about the principle of it and not specific details, then yes. I want you to put your feet up. But don't get too comfortable, okay? I still need my navigator."

"You'll always have me."

She shifted her gaze momentarily from the long stretch of highway in front of them to meet his. Romeo's green eyes glittered at her in the afternoon sunlight, and his smile made her think he wanted to say something more than the few words he'd chosen. "So." She had to look back at the road but not without regret. *That conversation's probably better for later, anyway.* "Did you find anything super interesting about this Ichacál place?"

He chuckled and glanced at his phone. "Yeah, actually. There was something about either an underground spring or a natural one that's supposed to have this really—"

With a loud thump and a crunch, the Winnebago rocked dangerously. Lily gritted her teeth and checked both side mirrors to be sure no one was driving behind them on the highway before she eased on the brake and pulled over to the shoulder. "Did that sound like I hit something?"

Romeo grimaced. "Maybe, yeah."

"Crap." She threw the gear into park and unbuckled her seatbelt.

"Wait, hold on." He studied the passenger side mirror and raised a hand. "Let me just check it out first."

"Hey, did you already forget what happened the last time you decided to check something out by yourself?"

He shot her a glance that clearly said she was overreacting. "I didn't forget anything. I simply wanna make sure there's nothing hiding out waiting to snatch you out from under my nose."

"Under your nose, huh?" They smirked at each other. "I appreciate the principle behind what you said, but if there's something out there, it's better for both of us that I'm there to fight it." Before he could protest, she yanked on the handle and shoved the door open into the unbearably hot afternoon.

With a sigh, he opened his door too, stepped out, and walked around the front of the Winnie. "Can you see what it was?"

"I see something in the road. I guess I kept driving for a while but I didn't hit a person, did I?"

"Lily, we definitely would've seen a person standing in the middle of the highway. It's probably only a stray dog or something."

"Oh, yeah. That's way better." They backtracked in the dry, dusty heat until they reached the dark form Lily had seen from the RV. "Gross."

Romeo frowned at the severed rabbit's head lying in the dirt and the bloody smear behind it. "You know, I don't think I've ever seen roadkill quite like that."

"What, a rabbit?"

"No. Without the rest of its body."

Lily grimaced and searched the surrounding highway. "Huh. Yeah, where is it?" They moved a few yards back the way they'd come and spun in slow circles to look for a headless rabbit corpse. "You know, I saw the head way up near the RV. The rest of it should be a lot easier to find than—"

Romeo uttered a low, furious snarl.

She almost told him not to get himself all worked up like that but noticed his tense stance and his attention focused beyond the highway. Her gaze settled on three women who walked toward them. They were still too far away for her to see their faces, but she knew in her bones these were the same dark-skinned women who'd been with Hugo at the disgusting fight ring.

Romeo uttered an even lower growl. "That's how I knew something was seriously wrong with that pack."

"Yeah. I know."

He glanced quickly at her. "You can smell them too?"

"No. But I can feel them. Those definitely aren't witches."

"They're not wolves, either."

"Well, I'm reasonably sure we can rule out vampires too—"

In an instant, the three women had leapt the dozens of yards between their position and the highway. Their sudden appearance in front of the two friends elicited a gust of wind that ruffled their hair and kicked tiny dust storms up around them. "What the—"

"We've come for you." Three voices spoke the identical words in unison, but none of the women's mouths moved.

"Nice try." Romeo crouched a little lower. "I'm not going anywhere with you."

"We have no interest in you, werewolf." The women stepped toward the highway together and moved as one despite their separate bodies and their clearly distinct styles of dress—cargo pants and t-shirt, a maxi dress, and Daisy Dukes under what could barely be called a top. "But Lily Antony has something we think would suit us very well."

"Whatever it is," Lily said, "you won't get it."

"We did not ask or make a request. But we shall make you an offer."

"No thanks."

"Come with us, Lily Antony. We sense the power

within you—so much darkness yearning to be freed. We can give you everything you seek. Your heart's greatest desires and more power than you have ever imagined." Together, the women raised their arms in a lame attempt to beckon her into their embrace. "And in return, your blood will complete the circle of—"

"Okay. See, here's the thing. If any of you had bothered to do your research, you would've found that everything you said is a complete waste of both our time." She raised her palm and summoned a whirling, crackling fireball.

The women even blinked at her in unison. Their black eyes flashed an eerie yellow and stayed that way, trained on her. "Do you deny our offer, Lily Antony?"

"Uh, yeah. That's exactly what I'm doing."

"Then you leave us no choice." A howling wind erupted around the women, Romeo, Lily, and the highway. Black hair whipped wildly around three stoic, emotionless faces. They raised their arms toward the sky and threw their heads back.

"Romeo, I think now would be a really good time to start getting into wolf mode."

"What?" She didn't take her eyes off the black-haired women but sensed him shake his head. "I can't fight them."

"Why not?"

"They're...women."

The creatures elevated at least three feet and snapped their heads forward with a vicious, ear-splitting screech. Their jaws fell open impossibly wide and dropped lower and lower like their faces were made of taffy instead of flesh and blood.

"Those are definitely not women," Lily shouted.

"Crap." His clothes landed in the dirt on the highway with a speed borne of desperation before the black wolf padded to Lily's side and growled.

She glared at the floating creatures in front of them. "So are we doing this or not?"

They shrieked again and lunged forward. She delivered her fireball into the woman on the far left, who swung wildly off course. Romeo's first pounce dragged the creature on the right completely out of her levitation. Lily didn't have the time to see where they landed but his snarls and the woman's grunts of frustration were enough. She summoned her strongest attack spell—at least the strongest that she could predict and control—and drew the sparking red energy behind her to aim it at the third creature.

Unfortunately, she wasn't fast enough.

The woman who'd stood in the center of the threesome —who now hovered in her billowing maxi dress—shoved her palms toward Lily and the young witch stumbled back from the force of the attack. She skidded roughly across the highway and grunted. "That's gonna hurt tomorrow." She threw three of her red missiles at her assailant in rapid succession. The first missed, the second grazed the woman's shoulder, and the third struck her squarely in the chest.

Romeo's powerful jaws snapped on thin air beside her. She turned quickly enough to see him land on all four paws again after an attempt at another upward lunge. The dark-skinned women regrouped, and when they rose again into the air and spread their arms, the air around them in the desert filled with something so that felt so incredibly wrong, Lily couldn't breathe for a few seconds.

"We will not be denied!" the women screamed as one before they hurtled into a combined attack.

A dark shadow burst across the highway and over the young couple's heads. Massive black wings stretched wide in an intimidating span. Dark tendrils trailed behind the bird-shaped shadow that now descended upon them. Lily prepared to launch an attack at it, fueled by Romeo's warning growls beside her, but the winged shadow apparently wanted nothing to do with her.

Instead, it swooped upon the three creatures who shuddered in the sky with their arms uplifted. She couldn't tell whether the black bird actually attacked the women or if it merely got close enough to scare them away. But a last terrified, furious shriek left three throats at once, and the dark-haired women vanished completely. A second later, the huge shadow dissipated and its last few strings of curling smoke gave way to the dry, bright heat of the Allende Valley and Mexico's Highway 450D.

The desert fell silent again. Slowly, Lily pushed herself to her feet, dusted herself off a little, and turned to search for another attack. There was none, fortunately, and Romeo growled and padded toward her before he stopped at her side. It didn't even occur to her that this was a serious first when she placed her hand on his head and dug her fingers into the coarse black hair slightly warmed by the sun. "Now, I'm really starting to think the shadow bird and the black heron are two completely different things."

He merely panted in response. "Okay. Come on. But keep an eye out, yeah?"

He moved silently down the highway beside her. Lily paused only to scoop his clothes off the road, bundled them in her arms, and returned quickly to the Winnie parked on the shoulder. When she stepped through the side door, she dropped his clothes on the cushy armchair beside it and continued to the driver's seat.

"That was seriously creepy." Romeo pulled his boxers and shorts on quickly and took his shirt with him to the passenger seat. "What the hell did they mean by 'your blood will complete the circle?'"

"I have no idea." Lily started the engine and pulled the Winnie onto their southward route. "I like my blood right where it is. And I won't make deals with anyone unless it gets me to my mom." When he had tugged his shirt over his head and back where it belonged, he buckled his seatbelt and caught her hand. She squeezed his, took a deep breath to clear all the craziness out of her head, and gave him a quick smile. "I gotta say, I really do like fighting with you. Not fighting you. I only mean...as a team."

He grinned at her. "I think you're awesome too."

TWENTY-EIGHT

Seven hours later, they'd settled into their campsite in the Sierras de Órganos national park in Zacatecas. They did have the ability to park the Winnie and stay overnight, but the amenities for RVs were a little more limited than they were used to. The park itself was stunning, with huge, natural pillars of rock thrusting into the orange-and-pink sky of sunset.

They lay together on a blanket stretched over the ground, which had slightly more greenery than the open valley in Chihuahua. The rock columns provided enough shade when the sun was high but now, in the mountains, the evening air before the light vanished completely was much cooler. Lily snuggled closer to Romeo with her head on his chest, and he held her as they watched what they could of the sunset's colors fading slowly into black.

He sighed. "Our first night completely alone in Mexico. It's hard not to appreciate that, huh?"

"And the picnic. That was a good idea for dinner

even if we technically still used the kitchen." She looked at him and drew her arm up his chest to play with the curls at the base of his neck. "Do you think you can keep from running around out here in the middle of the night?"

He laughed. "Hey, for now, I think I've had enough solo exploring as a wolf. I think I might go with the tried-and-true 'don't start any trouble for a while' method. I won't leave you. Promise."

"Good. I like waking up with you next to me, you know. Not having to go look for you is an extra bonus."

"Okay, okay. Point taken."

When the sun went down completely and the sky darkened fully, they had the most stunning view of the stars where they lay, punctuated by the rising rock columns around them. "They're so bright down here."

"That's what you get in the mountains. The closest town is still a few hours away. At least, the closest town that would have enough light pollution. You know, my dad and I went camping up in Boone one time—in the mountains too. I'd never seen so many stars up there. This beats that by a long shot."

"I'm only glad it cooled off. I honestly didn't think that was possible in Mexico."

He laughed. "I have a feeling we're gonna find many things here we didn't think were possible."

"Oh, yeah? Like what?"

Romeo rolled toward her onto his side and propped his head in his hand. "Well, for starters..." He glanced around and wiggled his eyebrows. "There's enough light from the stars for me to be a hundred percent sure that we're completely alone right now."

Lily grinned. "That's a good start. But merely because we don't see something doesn't mean it's not there."

"True." He trailed his fingers down her cheek. "I don't hear anything but bugs and birds." He tilted his head as if to listen more closely. "Maybe a lizard." she laughed until his fingers brushed the side of her neck and over her collarbone. "You wanna know what else makes me know we're alone?"

Closing her eyes, Lily focused on the shiver that rippled through her when his fingers drew a slow, sensual line down her chest, over her ribcage, and down past her belly. "Yeah."

"The only magic I smell here is yours."

"Well." She licked her lips when he teased her again and brushed his fingers under the top of her shorts and over her hipbone. "I'd say you almost have me convinced." It came out as a breathless whisper. He wound his arm around her waist and drew her under him on the blanket. She embraced him and kissed him in the starlight, thinking this was definitely the best way to spend their first night alone in Mexico.

A DOZEN yards away in Lily's Winnebago, the wooden box her mom had left her in Melissa Bore's magical vault rested on the kitchen counter. All on its own, the golden latch slid free and the lid creaked slowly open on its hinge. Inside, nestled between the poignantly relevant note and the few thousand dollars in solid gold coins, the stone-carved face from the Ichacál temple in Guatemala shuddered. It rocked from side to side within the few inches of space the box provided.

Finally, the stone drew itself upright until it stood fully erect and stopped moving. In the darkness of the Winnebago in the mountains of Zacatecas, Mexico, the dark eyes and open mouth in the stone face illuminated with an eerie, sickening green light. The glow brightened until it pulsed with powerful energy and filled the RV with a flash of brilliant green that swept over everything.

In the next moment, the light disappeared. The witch and werewolf on the blanket in the dirt never saw a thing.

With only a creepy stone idol as their next clue, Lily and Romeo are off again, this time taking the Winnebago through Mexico to Guatemala's healing temple of Ichacál in Any Witch Way.

Get sneak peeks, exclusive giveaways, behind the scenes content, and more.
PLUS you'll be notified of special **one day only fan pricing** on new releases.

Sign up today to get free stories.

CLICK HERE

or visit: https://marthacarr.com/read-free-stories/

For Hire: Teachers for special school in Virginia countryside.

Must be able to handle teenagers with special abilities.

Cannot be afraid to discipline werewolves, wizards, elves and other assorted hormonal teens.

Apply at the School of Necessary Magic.

AVAILABLE AT AMAZON RETAILERS

Find the compass, save the world or save herself?

Dating is harder for Maggie Parker than running down a felon. Now add in magic.

Did she just see a compass fly?

Can she learn how to use the magic of bubbles to chart a new course in time? It's a lot harder than it sounds.

Join her on her quest to rescue passengers on an ancient ship – a big blue marble called Earth – and save herself.

AVAILABLE ON AMAZON AND IN KINDLE UNLIMITED!

Two different writer friends repeated online this week something I spouted out to them last year and at a moment when I was the one who needed a reminder. In the spirit of passing this vibe along – I'll say it here again. I could even stand to press the point home for myself just a little more. Okay, here goes.

The Universe, with a capital U, loves you and has your back. Everything that happens is conspiring to help you out. I know, I know, it doesn't seem like that a lot of the time. Let me break it down for you.

I call the energy swirling all around us – *the Universe* - because I see us all as connected on this side and the next. Feel free to insert your own word or words. Science has already shown that we are big bodies of electricity putting out different frequencies. (The movie *I Am* by Tom Shadyac is a great documentary with a lot more about that – available on Amazon Prime.)

Okay, so we say or pray or write down in a journal the

things we hope to happen in our lives. Get a better job, find someone to love, even to just be happy. Great goals. But, in order to get there, we have to let go of what's not working for us anymore. The very things we're doing over and over again, so often we no longer notice that it's getting in the way of that goal. Like me telling myself I'm better behind the scenes than out front.

The Universe answers with opportunities to heal that inner hole, but to us it can look like things have gone from bad to worse. Like being out in front and not sure if a project like The Peabrain Society will work. Unless...

We can take a breath and stop pushing away at the very thing we didn't want to see and ask, "What are you here to teach me?" We stop being afraid of some idea that we see as a dark truth and become willing to listen. It's a simple idea that's tough to pull off – nearly impossible on our own. It usually takes a tribe of people willing to steer us back toward the solutions over and over again. And we do that for them as well. I start to break things down to just one day at a time and become kinder to myself and everyone around me.

I know it sounds like that movie, The Secret, but it's kind of not because there's a really practical part to all of this. We have to choose to go first and be brave every day and try. Make the phone calls, or go on that date, or show up at the gym, or forgive that person or ourselves. Whatever is on that list.

But, little by little, with someone saying, "You're doing fine, give it another day," we keep going, building our dream bit by bit as we let go of what was in the way.

Here's the last little part of this. If I can accept that the Universe loves me and has my back, then I don't need to protect against failure or doom, and I can create and build something. It doesn't mean I can't get knocked to my knees – I can and I have – it means that even that is part of building toward creation and my life is expanding, not shrinking. And it will be the doing that proves it to me on a cellular level, not the talking about it. Be brave fellow travelers and set out. I'm cheering for you all the time. More adventures to follow.

THANK YOU for not only reading this story but these *Author Notes* as well.

(I think I've been good with always opening with "thank you." If not, I need to edit the other *Author Notes*!)

RANDOM (*sometimes*) THOUGHTS?

About thirty (15) years ago I took some sales classes from a Sandler trainer (a well known sales training group.) After this training (or before, my memory sucks) I had picked up a sales training book that was written in the first third of the 20th century, so almost a hundred years ago.

This book (which I can't remember the name to) had very nearly the same training discussions and insights.

Before email, before TV, Before Radio I think. No Internet, no Videos... No international airplane travel.

Basically, people were people no matter the technology

around them, and you sold products the exact same way, but with way more touch points.

I remember this because no matter how advanced we (as a group) have become, as humans we really haven't changed much.

The absolute best way to sell someone is word of mouth. It's one of the reasons we (as authors) LOVE when you talk about our books.

(I'm stopping here - this wasn't meant to become a request for any support - just a thought.)

So, skipping books - if you happen to have a drink you like, suggest someone try it and find out if you have similar tastes.

Who knows, you might become like Ben and Jerry and decide to build an ice cream business.

AROUND THE WORLD IN 80 DAYS

One of the interesting (at least to me) aspects of my life is the ability to work from anywhere and at any time. In the future, I hope to re-read my own *Author Notes* and remember my life as a diary entry.

Shanghai, China

Twenty-ninth floor, somewhat corner suite. I'm working in the living room and Judith is asleep in the bedroom (it is 12:35AM in the morning.)

I've just finished a quick and dirty video-cast with Craig Martelle related (we hope) to success in your publishing business for the Facebook Group 20Books-to50k® where I totally interjected Martha Carr's name.

It had to do with her pushing through 30 years of publishing and found the highest success at year 30 (she had plenty of other success, just not the one she was looking for lately.) Martha, if you did not know it, is looked upon in our industry as an almost quasi-Zen teacher for many in our community.

I think Craig and I got side-tracked a bit in the be-live event. In fact, I KNOW we got side tracked because I was the side-tracker for many of the messed up parts of the conversation.

Martha, if you are reading this KNOW that I explained what I talked about so you wouldn't be COMPELLED to go listen to the video to find out what I said.

I totally just saved you 1/2 an hour of your life. You can thank me by wishing me Happy Birthday ON THE CORRECT DAY!

(Last year, she had all sorts of people on Facebook wishing me Happy Birthday week(s) early. It was not fun.)

FAN PRICING

$0.99 Saturdays (new LMBPN stuff) and $0.99 Wednesday (both LMBPN books and friends of LMBPN books.) Get great stuff from us and others at tantalizing prices.

Go ahead, I bet you can't read just one.

Sign up here: http://lmbpn.com/email/.

HOW TO MARKET FOR BOOKS YOU LOVE

Review them so others have your thoughts, tell friends and the dogs of your enemies (because who wants to talk with enemies?)... *Enough said ;-)*

Ad Aeternitatem,

Michael Anderle

OTHER BOOKS BY MARTHA CARR

Series in the Oriceran Universe:

SCHOOL OF NECESSARY MAGIC
SCHOOL OF NECESSARY MAGIC: RAINE
CAMPBELL
ALISON BROWNSTONE
THE DANIEL CODEX SERIES
THE LEIRA CHRONICLES
I FEAR NO EVIL
FEDERAL AGENTS OF MAGIC
THE UNBELIEVABLE MR. BROWNSTONE
REWRITING JUSTICE
THE KACY CHRONICLES
MIDWEST MAGIC CHRONICLES
SOUL STONE MAGE
THE FAIRHAVEN CHRONICLES

Other series:

THE LAST VAMPIRE

OTHER BOOKS BY JUDITH BERENS

OTHER BOOKS BY MARTHA CARR

JOIN THE ORICERAN UNIVERSE FAN GROUP ON FACEBOOK!

CONNECT WITH THE AUTHORS

Martha Carr Social

Website: http://www.marthacarr.com

Facebook: https://www.facebook.com/
groups/MarthaCarrFans/

Michael Anderle Social

Michael Anderle Social
Website:
http://www.lmbpn.com

Email List:
http://lmbpn.com/email/

Facebook Here: https://www.
facebook.com/TheKurtherianGambitBooks/